ABOUT THE AUTHOR

Joobin Bekhrad is the founder and Editor of *REORIENT*, an acclaimed publication about the contemporary arts and culture of the Middle East. He has also contributed to other publications, such as *The Cairo Review of Global Affairs*, *The Guardian*, *Anthropology of the Middle East*, *Encyclopaedia Iranica*, *Christie's*, and *Harper's Bazaar Art Arabia*, been interviewed by news outlets including *Newsweek* and the CBC, and seen his writings republished in a wide variety of languages.

In 2015, Joobin was granted an International Award for Art Criticism (IAAC) by London's Royal College of Art. He is also the author of a translation of Omar Khayyam's poems from Persian into English, as well as a foreword to Mahdi Ehsaei's *Afro-Iran*.

COMING DOWN AGAIN

Joobin Bekhrad

Copyright © 2016 Joobin Bekhrad

The moral right of the author has been asserted.

Apart from any fair dealing for the purposes of research or private study, or criticism or review, as permitted under the Copyright, Designs and Patents Act 1988, this publication may only be reproduced, stored or transmitted, in any form or by any means, with the prior permission in writing of the publishers, or in the case of reprographic reproduction in accordance with the terms of licences issued by the Copyright Licensing Agency. Enquiries concerning reproduction outside those terms should be sent to the publishers.

Matador
9 Priory Business Park,
Wistow Road, Kibworth Beauchamp,
Leicestershire. LE8 0RX
Tel: 0116 279 2299
Email: books@troubador.co.uk
Web: www.troubador.co.uk/matador
Twitter: @matadorbooks

ISBN 978 1785899 447

British Library Cataloguing in Publication Data.
A catalogue record for this book is available from the British Library.

Printed by Printed and bound in the UK by TJ International, Padstow, Cornwall
Typeset in 12pt Bembo by Troubador Publishing Ltd, Leicester, UK

Matador is an imprint of Troubador Publishing Ltd

ACKNOWLEDGMENTS

I am eternally indebted to my parents, Tirajeh Tehranchian and Shahdad Bekhrad; without their support, neither would this book have come to fruition, nor would I be where I am today. I am also thankful to Mahvash Tehranchian, my grandmother, who kept asking whether I'd finished writing this yet, and Tiraneh Tehranchian, my aunt, for all her advice.

I would also like to thank Tina Gharavi, Tom Holland, and Hooman Majd for taking the time to read my manuscript and provide me with encouraging feedback, as well as Mélodie Hojabr Sadat for her beautiful illustrations and Rahill Jamalifard for her touching introduction. A thank you is also owed to my friends Emine Gözde Sevim, Inaya Hodeib, and Rania Moudaress for their uplifting and reassuring words.

FOREWORD

Rahill Jamalifard

God knows how many times my father used to recite the poems of Hafez and Sa'di, over and over, blindly hoping that I, a fourteen-year-old first-generation Iranian-American, would at once comprehend the meaning of our most sacred texts. I desired to surpass his hopes to prove that I, too, had been sewn from the same fabric of these poets, that I, too, had been forged in the flames of love, lust, and desire. Alas, it didn't come easily; my father had to spend hours taking apart words and explaining their symbolism, and teaching me the history required for understanding each and every *ghazal*. The sad truth is that I grasped very little of my father's lessons. Halfway through his longwinded explanations, my curiosity and interest would dissipate; I'd start thinking about school and art, and above all, the songs that never stopped playing in my mind.

 Music. Music was a whole other story. My father would sit me down on our couch and play me songs by Delkash and Kourosh Yaghmaei; and, without any explanation, as if we were both listening to the anthems of our souls, we would sit together, united and captivated by the voices coming from the cassette player. He didn't have to tell me anything about the poems they were singing, because I could *feel* them; my heart would swell with emotion, and I understood their pain and sadness. This bond between my father and me was forged through these emotive melodies, which we both connected to at once, and that brought us a special kind of joy.

Perhaps this is why I can relate completely to Joobin's story of Asha, an angst-ridden teenager growing up in Tehran, the notoriously bustling capital of Iran. As Asha began scouring the ends of his own domain to unearth all things rock and roll, playing dress-up in his mother's clothes and trying to be just like Keith Richards, I – on the other side of the world – dug through my father's collection of dubbed VHS tapes, filled with footage of Iranian music programmes from the 70s. Asha's narration takes me back to that time; there is a familiarity in his words, and one can't help but relate to his love for the girl next door, his rejection, and his self-discovery. His trumping desire to escape a city he loves, but feels imprisoned in at the same time, to pursue his dream of becoming a rock star in London, echoes the trials of every youth coming of age. Asha's emotional dilemmas and malaises, which are seemingly only alleviated through music, highlight the comfort and companionship that I and so many like me have found in records and tapes. Just as the sound of Keith's guitar and David Bowie's image soothe Asha's aching heart, so has Nico's sombre voice healed mine.

Asha, Joobin's discontented young nonconformist, finds solace and a means of self-expression through the power and promise of rock and roll. With his electric guitar, records, and music videos, he is able to find his own freedom, and an imaginary ticket out of the tumultuous relationship he has with Tehran, the only city he's ever known. I reconnected with my own teenage years when reading about the adventures of Asha, who also gives an honest narration of what Tehran feels like in the sneakers of a love-stricken schoolboy. In his own words, he accustoms readers with a historic and cultural rhetoric intertwined with vernacular Persian and slang, and puts them, too, in the blazing heat of a summer's afternoon in Tehran. Listening with Asha to the sounds of traffic and passers-by on Cypress Lane amidst the smell of instant coffee, one can only hope that he will ultimately find his way to London with his cherry-red electric guitar as not Asha the heartbroken teenager, but Asha the Hound, the 'shaggy Persian punk-poet wrought of fire and stone'.

New York City, 2016

Rahill Jamalifard is an NYC-based artist and lead singer of the American rock outfit Roya. A first-generation Iranian-American, her work often explores her relationship with her roots and how they shape her identity.

1

August, with her slow, burning afternoons and limpid dreams. August, a brief, bittersweet respite from the doldrums of strung-out schoolboy hours and watching eyes. August, and the blues.

They're at it again. I can see the oil-smeared labourers with gimlets for eyes through the haze of sandalwood smoke rising in Chinese clouds from a silver-toned lotus flower. The curls are mingling with a perpetual film of dust, accentuated by dots of fingerprints, as I sit here, looking out into the distance from behind my rotting white windowsill. The Stones are on VH1 Classic again, I've had my third cup of bitter black instant coffee, and I don't know what to do today, as usual. Mum and Dad are out; there's only me, the workers, my simian saviours on the television, a dog-eared English paperback about rock and roll, and my battered cherry-red guitar.

Ghermezi, my electric guitar, is perhaps my most prized possession. I remember vividly the day I brought her home, bundled up in cardboard and Styrofoam in the back of a dirty old Paykan taxicab. I was walking around Jomhuri Avenue in my tattered canvas sneakers with Arezu on my mind, ogling the sundry electric guitars hanging in the vitrines of the stores lining the bustling street. There were candy-coloured Strats and Teles as far as my teenage eyes could see, but none of them caught my interest. They were too common; everyone had one, and I wanted something *different*. It was only when I was about to head back home that I espied, through the door of a little shop reeking of sweat and mothballs and brimming with hot bodies in blue jeans, what I believed to be the holy grail of guitars. Reclining demurely against a shiny black stand, its dulled, chipped body and weathered neck beckoned me to come closer and push my way through the throng of spiky-haired teenagers. Upon closer inspection, it seemed the vicissitudes of time had, over the years, turned its once-white plastic pickguard a sickly shade of yellow. One could barely make out the numbers on its black-ridged knobs, and the spot where a proud decal once rested had been reduced to a smattering of specks that shone in dreamy, pearly tones. It looked just like the one I'd once imagined a piratic Keith Richards bandying around in striped trousers on *Brown Sugar*; I don't know why, but I always pictured that guitar to be bright red and white, gleaming like some kind of creamy, candied delicacy. *Yes, you could be mine,* I thought to myself as cool droplets streaked down my sides, *tonight, and every night.*

If there's one thing I know in this life, it's that I want to be a rock and roll star. One day, some day, I will throw Ghermezi over my shoulder, board a big jet plane, and head for London, the greatest city in the world, to make it big with my band. I've even chosen a name for it: The Afghan Hounds. Yes, I shall be Asha the Hound, the shaggy Persian punk-poet wrought of fire and stone, who can make his guitar howl filthier than anyone else. I long to be let loose on the streets of London, where I'll bark and growl and paint the town red. There's just no place in this city for a rock and roller, for longhaired boys who see the world through stardust, glitter, leopard prints, and dazzling flashes of light. There's no place for us here in this tulip-strewn realm cradled in the mountains, on these bloodied streets beneath the gazes of ghosts and black billows.

I can make it there as a rock star; over there, I can be anything I want. But then again, I don't know what else I can do other than give a guitar a good thrashing. I wouldn't mind being like the guy in *Blow-Up*, which Jamshid and I saw the other day over soda and cheese puffs. He had it nice, driving around in posh cars in smart clothes, snapping pictures of models, didn't he? I don't know the first thing about working a camera, though, and, quite frankly, would much rather smash a guitar to pieces like Jeff Beck. Writing about rock and roll, I suppose, is something I could also try my hand at. I'm quite enjoying, for all its drabness, the decomposing copy of *Pop, Rock, and Soul* I snagged at the old Hyatt hotel the other week with Jamshid. But who wants to sit down and *write* about rock and roll when you can be a guitar god? I like my notes loud and fuzzy.

That, pretty much, only leaves old cherry-red here, aside from whom I've never cared for much else – except Arezu, the pretty girl on the fifth floor who smells of cotton candy and flowers, and who will never be mine. If I don't get out of this flat and this city, I'll either waste away from boredom or heartbreak. 'Degh kard!' they'll say, when they open my door to find a scrawny heap of bones, crowned like a cock, clutching a guitar. I love Arezu, but she's recently hit it off with that boor Babak, whose balls are always bursting through the buttons of his boutique blue jeans. You'd never believe that Babak, the boy who sits behind me in calculus class, is the son of beardless Haji Hosseini, one of Tehran's most notorious mullahs; but I'm used to such contradictions now. I see them walking together, sometimes alone, sometimes with other sweet things, from behind the window of our living room, crouching behind the couch lest they see me. The poets were right to curse the heavens; what does he have that I don't? Muscles, perhaps, money, and a shiny, finely chiselled nose that seemingly diminishes in size with time. Yes, as hard as it is to digest, Arezu has chosen Hasselhoff over Hendrix. Some people have no taste. *Akh*, Ghermezi, it's just you and me against the world.

2

Coffee, coffee, and more coffee. I'm starting to get the jitters, but I fancy another cup of the black stuff nonetheless. If you were to slit open my veins, you'd find more coffee and beer in me than anything else; I suppose it's what you could call a rock star diet. Why can you get as much coffee as you want here, while beer is harder to come by? I can't stand the flavoured rubbish they sell on the streets, although it's not every day that the men on bikes with brown paper bags brimming with bitter German lager come around to Jamshid's place. It's true – if you've got money, you can get anything you want here: booze, drugs, sex, music, movies. With a house in Velenjak and fistfuls of *tomans*, you wouldn't want for anything; you might even like it. But, alas, there are some things here not even Khomeini's hallowed visage can buy.

I've never really thought about how large a part of my day quaffing cups of instant coffee consumes. It isn't because I'm a caffeine junkie, though; blame it on this boredom. When Jamshid isn't around, I sit here on this garish sofa with legs splayed, watching scrambled satellite television and movies I ask Blind Bahman to find for me (he isn't really blind – we just call him that because of his tiny eyes). Making coffee during these lazy days is an event, a ritual, a spectacle, almost. Not only does it afford the exercise of getting up from the couch to drag my skinny arse to the kitchen, but also a moment of contemplation. As the hot water mixes with those insipid brown crystals, I ponder how I'm going to kill time and while away the rest of the day, and think about how many more of this damned summer are left before the bullshit begins again. Either that, or I think about Arezu while my bowels writhe about.

The satellite's working again; no more is the world a hodgepodge of squeaks, pips, and purple. Bryan Ferry's on the television singing *Avalon*, and the nauseatingly ambient chord changes aren't helping this jelly-like feeling within in the slightest; they're only making Arezu's image appear even brighter before my eyes. Lovesickness and melancholy melodies are not to be mixed, it seems; I was much happier when Parliament-Funkadelic was on. Roxy Music is far more entertaining, I would argue, than being told in Arabic that I'm going to burn in hell, or listening to some constipated cleric respond to marital issues on a hotline.

I need to get out of this house, out of these four walls weighing so heavily upon my soul, but have nowhere to go. Jamshid's out, God knows where, and it's so stiflingly hot outside that sometimes, I'm just tempted to throw myself on my bed and shut my eyes beneath the cool breeze and buzz of the new Korean air conditioner we've just installed. Sometimes I feel so lonely here, so desperate, that I even miss the tedium of school and the autumn rains. Burdon's voice is burning in my brain: *We gotta get outta this place, if it's the last thing we ever do.* When, *ey Khoda*, when will this summer ever end?

3

The Father: Cyrus
The Most Badass Son-of-a-Gun to Have Ever Walked the Earth: Keith Richards
The Holy Spirit: Zoroaster

Such is the triumvirate my scrawny teenage self pledges fealty to. Theirs are the first countenances I see when I arise from my slumbers, and the last, when, broken down by the boredom of these boiling afternoons, I slip beneath the sheets of my little bed. Ever since, many moons ago, Auntie Niku let me have the copy of *Sticky Fingers* I found in her decomposing tape collection, I've wanted to be Mister Keith Richards more than any other rock star—even Freddie. He's my style guru, my guitar god, my *raison d'être.* Mum and Dad aren't particularly crazy about my rooster-do (circa 1969), and think I bear more semblance to a creature in a menagerie than a sixteen-year-old boy, but I don't care; I want to rock like Keith, walk like Keith, and talk like Keith. If I cock my head at the right angle and look in the mirror from my 'better' side (i.e. the one from which my nose doesn't appear as bony and oblong), I fancy I look quite a bit like him. It's only finding the clothes, though, that has proven difficult here in Tehran. They don't sell leopard print shirts at the Tajrish Bazaar.

When my parents are out, I sometimes venture into their room to raid Mum's closet and play dress-up, so mind-numbing is my ennui. There, all by myself, surrounded by Mum's colourful clothes, I let my imagination run wild, throwing on myself every manner of sumptuous shawls, billowing trousers, frilly shirts, and all. Oh, if only I could strut around the squalid streets of Tehran dressed as a pirate! How sweet, then, would life be. I've got the hair, at least, which took me a proper year to cultivate into a jumble even Johnny Thunders would be proud of, and I'll be damned if any black-booted *pasdar* gets it in his head to give me a trim. Last week, my classmate Kambiz was caught at a party bustling with birds drinking hooch, and they did a number on his head in the slammer. Kambiz *kachal* the kids call him now; Kambiz, who once sported a Farrokhzad 'fro. By God, I'll take to the streets if they ever lay a finger on me and my cherished *kakol*.

It's not all that boring, being left to yourself to doff your sweats and emerge from Mum's magic closet as a rock star. I try on her turquoise rings and necklaces, unbutton her rippled blouses down to my navel, tie a sash around my waist, daub a splash of *kohl* on my lashes, and, with my guitar slung way down low, upheld by a cord of cracked leather, look in the mirror and behold myself, a redoubtable twentieth century boy, in all my gaudy glory. With *Goat's Head Soup* (the *kaleh pacheh* album, as I like to call it) blasting from my stereo at just the right volume so as to not bring Khanum Bahrami downstairs and bang on the door, I'm as happy as any caged bird can be, far from faded tulips, clouds of smog, the sultry gazes of the girls on Vali-ye Asr, and the looming threat of the morrow. Inevitably, though, my dance with Mr. D comes to an end, and I'm left standing in my bedroom in Mum's satin shirt with Ghermezi in my sweaty hands, wondering how to while away the rest of the day and kill the hours left yet.

4

Usually, during such bathetic hours, there's a handful of ways I can busy my spiritless self. I can always pour myself a cup of coffee, kick back my spindly legs on the garish sofa, and dream about the wily, windy moors of England lauded by a wide-eyed Kate Bush in falsettos on VH1 – if the station isn't scrambled, of course. There are also books, dog-eared and awash with the sublime, ineffable scent of childhood dreams rising forth from their yellowed pages. At the moment, I've got my long bony nose in *Rock, Pop, and Soul* (the pictures are better than the text) and the *Upanishads*, which Jamshid has lent me. Jamshid's either smoking grass, drinking beer, or reading 'heavy' books, which he bangs on about with fervour underneath the dusty picture of Beckett at Khosrow's café, our usual haunt. I don't read enough, Jamshid says; and, as he did with beer and grass, he's now trying to turn me on to books and philosophy.

Books only interest me to the extent that they pertain to rock stars and their guitars; otherwise, nothing gets my juices flowing like my records. Whoever said the pen is mightier than the sword obviously hadn't heard the scream of a fuzzed-out electric guitar. Give me Bowie over that birdman Beckett any day. Who would want to be some dried-up philosopher sitting on his arse and racking his brain when they could be like Ziggy? I can't fathom how Jamshid can spend hours on end puffing on the green stuff and flipping page after page. I told Jamshid fiction was bullshit the other day, to which, as we walked down the alley with the mural of the hot air balloon, he responded that there is much truth to be found in it, perhaps even more so than in reality. Some day, he says with a smile, I will see the method to his madness and, like him, find solace in stanzas and strophes beneath a canopy of stars. I tell him that they will sooner hold an open-air rock concert in Azadi Square.

Sometimes at Jamshid's place, when my hirsute host retires to the kitchen to brew a frothy pot of sweet Turkish coffee, I gaze, glassy-eyed, at the scores of tomes bursting from every nook and cranny in his stuffy flat. I wonder if it's only me, or if the sight of brimming bookshelves gets everyone antsy down under. I've never been able to linger long in bookstores or libraries; I always end up having to make a dash for the loo to purge my insides. All those rows of thick, wrinkled spines emblazoned with the names of giants, sitting solemnly under blankets of soot and dust, remind me of how little I know, and how little I am (just like school). I pick up a book, flip to a page at random, and read a few lines that give my head a proper spin. I feel at times as if I'm the only person who doesn't understand these words and passages, and that I'll never be as learned as Jamshid; but, then again, Jamshid can't work an electric guitar like I can. The mere thought brings consolation in warm waves.

5

I can't be bothered to read now, though; I've just ploughed through a chapter on glam rock, on Bowie, Bolan, and all those cats, and have had my fill for the day. Come to think of it, I can't be arsed to do anything except lie here on my stomach in the thick glow of the afternoon sun, listening to the sound of crows, children on the dusty avenue, and, from afar, the call to prayer. Where's Jamshid when you need him? Only he can bring me to my senses now. I might even go to Khosrow's alone, for the mere sake of getting out of this house caving in on me. One of the great things about this city is that everything takes so long, and requires so much effort, that it becomes a project. Mr. and Mrs. Aryanpour, our new neighbours, told us the other day that they returned from Toronto because they had nothing to do there; everything was too easy, too convenient. They missed, believe it or not, the mania of Tehran. But I don't want to go to Toronto; I want to go to London, to see the bright lights.

I wonder how long I can lie here, listening to the springs of my squeaky bed as my moist body writhes about on my pink pillow, made wet and warm by my breath. My arms have gone numb, my chin is beginning to ache, and I'm beginning to decipher all sorts of sounds in the cacophony outside my window, as if, like Solomon, I've been endowed with the language of the birds. So mired am I in this ennui that I don't even feel like strumming those slinky silver strings rotted by sweat and disillusionment in equal measure. All the while, I'm troubled by an unfathomable motion in the depths of my being, which ebbs and flows between my breast and backside. It soothes and singes at once, brings a bittersweet taste to my cheeks, and leaves me in a lather. There is hope yet, it whispers, while in warm flushes I'm reminded of the futility of it all. I've always been drawn to the impossible, to what can never be, what will never be mine, to faraway eyes.

Everywhere, her eyes. *Well, you know what kind of eyes she got.* Everywhere, in the smooth, sun-kissed visages of child martyrs, beneath Nasereddin's brows, in the faces flickering on the television in reds and blues. Burned in my mind are the curve of her smile and the flash of her lithe white neck, nestled in the serpentine folds of her headscarf. Does the girl on the fifth floor, who smells of cotton candy, know how she's burnt the little heart of this wretched one to ashes? How he scribbles poems on torn pages she will never read, songs on the back of tissues she will never hear? Of course she does, the heartless bitch; it's written all over his beet-red face. I wish I could be like Jamshid. He doesn't bother himself with birds; he keeps his nose in his books. He's lost faith in earthly love, he says. He's after the pure stuff. The key to the universe, Jamshid tells me, is in my own heart. I'm just not looking hard enough. What Jamshid doesn't understand, however, is that I'll always be a fool for pretty girls, as I've always been; for sleepless nights, clutching onto sticky sheets, tormented by the wounding gaze of some girl named after a flower while the world outside is still blanketed in bright blue hues. I don't mind if Jamshid laughs at me or calls me a *zan-zalil*; all I want is for Arezu to love me back.

Her eyes, now, seem further away than ever. For comfort, I sometimes try to delude myself by thinking she's not as pretty as I imagine, that there are loads of better-looking girls out there who might possibly, as hard as it is to fathom, make room for me within their hearts. This is, after all, Tehran, where pretty girls are anything but a rarity. My heart, however, has never been a thing to know reason, and has always been at odds with my head. From up yonder, beyond clouds imbrued with exhaust and woe, the colours of that countenance pour down, washing the faces of all and sundry with the stuff of tender illusions. I can see naught else: everything becomes *her*. I don't want the others, with their bandaged noses and beehives; I want her, whom I love and hate at once, the pretty girl with the long, bumpy nose who smells of cotton candy and bathes me in cool sweats, slipping, slowly but surely, through my bony hands.

Enough! Get up, Asha, put on your bright blue jeans and jet-black sneakers, take a swig of Johnnie, and hit the streets; the night is young, but fast fading. You don't need the sweet-smelling girl. Damn her and those eyes of hers. September is coming to snatch away our innocence, to bind us in fetters, to darken our days in autumnal dusk until Mithras rises again. Yes, *tonight* … tonight, I am Asha the Hound, ready to prowl the sordid streets of this city in search of cheap thrills and a bite to eat. I want the key to the universe. I want to break free of these four walls. I want to break someone's heart.

But I know, deep down, that all I want is her.

6

Chris *fucking* de Burgh. I loathe him even more than the Channel Two jingle. He was on the radio – again – and what was more worrying was that the driver was grooving to his every whine. Would a little Stones have been too much to ask for? Perhaps, in the spirit of the evening, something black, something blue, would have done; or, maybe a bit closer to home, some Queen for a good old-fashioned lover boy. I don't know why some think Western music has been banned here; everyone knows you can find any song you like, as long as it's schmaltz and you can't tap your feet to it. I don't think there's any other city in the world that can boast its own soundtrack, replete with songs that follow you wherever you go. There's no escape: taxis, cafés, elevators, bathrooms – they've all been sullied by what I call the 'Shit List':

Chris de Burgh – *Lady in Red*
Lionel Ritchie – *Hello*
Cat Stevens – *Father and Son*
The *Love Story* theme song (in every possible arrangement)
The *Titanic* theme song (in every possible arrangement)

No, you won't hear the likes of Keef, Johnny, and Ziggy anywhere near here. The closest one can get to rock and roll, if lucky, is the odd Pink Floyd number here and there, lurking in the shadows of some of the city's trendier cafés. That doesn't mean, however, that you can't get your hands on proper records; if there's one place you can find anything in, it's Tehran; all you have to do is to look in the right places, and ask the right people. It also helps to have friends and relatives who bring back the good stuff in cracked black suitcases from Europe and 'the other side of the water'. For rock and roll, Mad Manuch is my man; no sooner do I shove a wad of grubby *tomans* in my pocket than it finds its way into his hairy brown hands: a fine reward for a fine prize. At this rate, I'm not going to have anything saved up for London, where I'll need as much dough as I can get. Everything afforded me by birthdays and *Norooz* is fast blown on records, films, and shoes. What else does one need in life? The other week, Manuch found me copies of the Led Zeppelin best-of DVD and *The Rise and Fall of Ziggy Stardust and the Spiders from Mars*. One day I, too, will play the Royal Albert Hall with the Hounds. One day, I will see the cat from Japan.

* * *

The night smelled of crackling wild rue and cigarettes. She is a city to behold when the sun hides her face behind the mountains, Tehran. Glowing red neon, splashes of yellow light on dusty green leaves, pink lips, and Persian blue. A symphony of horns and curses, the clamour of children tugging at their mother's black chadors for the ice of idylls, the plaintive moans of a lone *ney* begging to be heard amongst the bustle of the boulevard. I have spent the whole of my short life here on these streets that shine beneath the moon, on sleepy Cypress Lane by the foothills of the snowcapped Alborz Mountains. I have known little else, only imagining in soft colours the wide, wild world beyond my window. My only solace, rock and roll, and my only saviour, love. With ardour in my breast and my weathered cherry-red guitar by my side, I can rise above these soot-stained buildings, above these mountains, above the damning glances and harangues that so haunt the halls. But where, love? Where, the sound of scalding rusted steel and weathered wood?

Again, that sinking feeling, the ethereal nausea of *Avalon. Perhaps I shouldn't have had that Zoghali burger,* I thought. The noxious admixture of fast food, Roxy Music, and the smog of waning summer hours had gotten me in a sweat. I rolled down the window and closed my eyes as a highland zephyr curled my tousled raven locks around its fingers. At the crimson countdown of the traffic lights, a sad-eyed waif offered me a rose in a blackened hand. My pity was accentuated by the realisation that I didn't have any purpose for the stuff of poets. I wanted to tell him that the girl with faraway eyes loves me not, and to try his luck elsewhere; but before I could, we lost him in a puff of exhaust as we sped up the hills towards the mountains. *I should have bought the rose*, I said to myself; but no, it was too late. He had been swallowed up by the night, by the faceless throng.

The burly driver popped in an old Ebi cassette in his detachable stereo and asked me where we were going. I didn't know; yet again, I was all dressed up and had no place to go, just a lonesome schoolboy on a hot summer night. I thought about how, if Arezu were with me, we'd go up, up, up in the mountains, steal away from the hysteria of the streets and the quietude of closed bedroom doors, and trace lines in the sky, losing ourselves in the mirrors of our eyes. I wondered where she was, imagining her with that lucky bastard who doesn't know what's hit him. One of these days, he'll come a-knockin' in black and white to ask her parents for her soft white hand, and it'll really be curtains for me, then. Why, out of all the doe-eyed girls in Tehran, did I have to fall in love with you, Arezu Atashi? But you, like me, sprung from the sunbaked soil of this city, know that we always want what can never be ours.

7

I remember now why I don't get out that often anymore: the memories. Everything in this confounded city reminds me of things I'd rather forget. Every district, teeming with childhood fears and worries, every alley, redolent of wasted days and nights. Here, the place where Arezu once smiled at me from behind the boughs of a broken plane tree, there, where her eyes met mine before she jumped on the faux leather seats of her father's white Paykan. Even the afternoon sun, between three and four, to be precise, reminds me of the agony of schoolboy trials, the horrors of homework, and the heavy-hearted walk back home through the dusty, flower-strewn corridors of our neighbourhood. Sometimes, I want to get away, far away, where nothing is familiar and no one knows my name. I want to burn, and from the ashes of my scorched childhood, arise anew. Rather, this city, this summer, those eyes, are burning me.

I don't know why I like that place, Niavaran, but I do. Perhaps it's because it's one of the few remaining places in Tehran that doesn't bring to mind any churning thoughts of yesterday, a virgin stretch of this concrete jungle. It's cooler there, greener, and closer to the mountains, those craggy thresholds between the mundane and the unknown. I've always wondered what lies beyond their creamy peaks, from which pours the draught of the heavens onto these scorched streets. I have yet to venture past them, let alone see that faraway isle whose visions loom large before my eyes. I know I will leave these mountains one day – of that I'm sure; but, I also know that, wherever I go, I will always walk within their shadows, those in which I was born on one cold, caliginous night in December's deep.

Mithras arose, then, from his winter slumber, to the sound of burnt-out guitars caked in lager and sweat aplenty. I am sure that, on that Eve of *Yalda*, in the little hospital Mum still points out whenever she drives past it, somewhere, somehow, the slinky dun reels of a Dolls tape must have been spinning away. It was that sound precisely, the sound that would brand its impression in my ears, that lured me away from the warmth of the womb, from which I, Asha, the Persian-born acolyte of love and light, emerged. I was a poet who knew not the language of the birds, a rocker to whose soft, vestal fingers were foreign the touch of cool, wiry steel; but it had been written on my forehead, and upon the pages of my heart, that which I was destined to be: a shaggy-haired, skinny thing longing for naught but the twang of his cherry-red guitar and Arezu's sleepy brown eyes.

Flashes of neon, bulbs of blue, and the green glow of the mosque: the place looked prettier than ever that night. I wanted to get lost in some lush backstreet, and think about nothing at all – not about school, not about the future, not about Arezu and Babak, not about getting out of this place, not about the *Upanishads,* not about whether Mad Manuch could find me that John Lennon album I'd asked him for. I wanted to turn off this damn thing in my head that's always frying away, always in overdrive. I wish I could be like Jamshid, happy in this city with my piles of novels and handfuls of grass, like Babak, who mustn't have a care in the world now that he's got Arezu in his bulging arms, or like … like these stray cats. People pity them, throw stones at them; I think it's because they're jealous. They're the luckiest creatures in this crazy city. They can do whatever they want, go wherever they please, ramble about without so much as a thought for the morrow. And they don't fall in love. Sometimes I wish I, too, were a tiny, tawny, blackened ball of fur that could take on the world with its little paws. *Oh yeah, you're a strange stray cat.* Perhaps in some other life, in some other world, if there is one.

Better out than in. Before me, mottled on the stained, crumbling tiles, were the bits and bobs of what had hours ago been a steamy, hot patty and ketchup-doused fries, courtesy of Zoghali Burger and Roxy Music. *I knew I was sick*, I said to myself. Fortunately, I hadn't stained my precious blue jeans, my only pair. They're torn and frayed all over, just like my Converse sneakers, and I wouldn't have it any other way. Of course, I could buy myself a few other pairs, but that wouldn't be punk. I saw someone wearing a t-shirt once that read, 'If it isn't cheap, it isn't punk'. I'll never forget that. I don't know what's written in Jamshid's books with portraits of bespectacled, bearded men on their covers, but I have always lived my life according to two philosophies:

Good thoughts, good words, and good deeds,
and
Five strings, three notes, two fingers, and one asshole.

How can you go wrong? Life, I sometimes think, is much simpler than most people have led us to believe. I don't want the things that other kids get off on – fast cars, loads of cash, and all the sex a randy sixteen-year-old could beg for. Is that happiness? I only want to play my guitar, for school to end, to get away from this city that raises me and brings me down, to never fall in love again. Is that too much to ask for? I've never wanted much, really.

8

Some follow the sun. I have always had my head in the clouds, have always looked to the empyrean for the smooth caress of Anahita's lithe, outstretched hands on my cheeks. I don't know why they say rain is depressing. There is a certain sadness to it, yes; but it is a sadness tinged with sweetness, an ambrosial sort of melancholy to those knowing, like that of teenage love, of the cloying warmth of Ferry's crooning. I've heard it rains quite often in England, that the sun seldom shows her face there. If so, then it must surely be Paradise on earth.

It was one of those rare summer nights in Tehran, the stuff of fantasy, when the city, awash with manna from up high, shines against the sky in a thousand different colours; one of those nights when, from the earth, imbrued with blood, rises forth the scent of tulips and clay, of the never-dead and never-born, of forgotten days of a bygone age. I felt like Keith Richards in *Waiting on a Friend*, except that no one was waiting for me in any doorway, and I'd never be half as cool as him. It was romantic at the outset, when the first drops slid down my neck, but I knew I'd soon be soaked to the bone if I didn't get inside somewhere fast. *Where do I go?* I asked myself. There wasn't a taxicab in sight, and the *garçons* wouldn't let me loiter about in a restaurant until the downpour died down. In any case, the dawn was far beyond the horizon, it was a Thursday night, and I'd have done anything to stay out of my room with all its pin-ups and avoid one of those dreaded chats about life with Mum and Dad at the dinner table. I remembered that Auntie Niku, who lives just a few blocks down the main drag in Niavaran, was probably around. She, like me, is always dressed up with no place to go, and knows well the taste of sorrows drowned in beer.

9

Auntie, down and out, looked like you could have wrung a bottle of cheap red wine out of her. While the rain laved the glowing, throbbing world down below, Googoosh sang on the television below a framed, faded picture of Zoroaster looking up unto Mazda, and Auntie lay supine on a little *gelim,* blowing clouds into the air. Sticking, lingering everywhere, was Auntie's saccharine rosewater perfume, the one that always reminds me of the sultry history teacher who once put me to task as a twelve-year-old. I like it there at Auntie's pad, nestled high above in the foothills of the mountains; I can do things I can't when Mum and Dad are around. It was there that I had my first drink, that I listened to my first rock and roll records, that kohl-eyed gods whispered in my ear and sank their stained yellow teeth into my virgin skin. But Auntie still won't let me touch the slim cigarettes whose ends she reddens with her painted lips, even though she knows I puff away on Bahmans in blue jeans when no one's looking.

There have only ever been two rock and rollers in the annals of the Soroushi family: Auntie and I. All the others have gone on to join the vapid crowds of myriad other doctors, engineers, and lawyers – the only 'respectable' professionals in this country. I've never cared much for being respectable, if that means being like everyone else. Mum and Dad are worried sick that they won't call their little boy 'Agha-ye Mohandes' one day, that his future wife won't, in front of her Botoxed friends, call him 'Doktor'. I'm just worried sick that I won't make it out of here in one piece, that they'll strip me of my beloved *kakol* and take away Ghermezi, that the Ministry of Guidance will have me on my knees begging for their blessings to shove muzak down people's throats, that I'll be there, in the band, to play the blues when Arezu and Babak tie the knot and seal my fate. I don't want to waste away in some little flat watching powdered, spectral faces, always lost, always wondering if – just maybe – there is something more than this.

Auntie doesn't play the guitar, but she's a rocker at heart: she drinks, smokes, and worships Freddie Mercury. Sometimes, when heady with thick purple wine, she becomes a child again and lets loose from the smoky caverns of her throat the songs of Delkash, the same ones she would sing on the rooftop as a child, before the sun set behind the mountains and the lion's scowl. I feel I can talk to Auntie about things; she isn't like Mum and Dad, always shaking their heads and scratching their faces in frustration. She says I'm meant for higher things, and that I will go places with my cherry-red guitar. Every now and then, I strum my songs for her in her living room, covered with tobacco-stained Persian rugs and soot-smeared satin, drenched in sweat, burning bright. Auntie's flat is the only stage I've ever known, and Auntie, the only fan. As heavy as these days and nights can feel, something in my little bones tells me I will, one day, under hot lights in Hammersmith, remember the mountains, my room, Auntie's smoky laughter, and the chronic nausea engulfing them all, and smile. It might even, perhaps, make for a good song.

Auntie poured me a much-needed draught of golden elixir and took another drag from a Winston. She was quiet, looking at boughs bent by the driving rain outside, while I kicked back on a tribal carpet, gazing at the burning end of her cigarette in the corner of my eye. Burning, always burning … and for what? Burning the midnight oil, scribbling down poems no one will ever read or hear, burning for pipe dreams of far-flung isles, burning the monotony of hours, days, and years, hoping in vain that something will change, eventually. But nothing has changed, nor will it; we are the children of war, of revolution, of the burnt generation, beaten down and fizzled out, but full of blood yet. Life, for us, is simple when you think about it. We only have two options: we either get out of here, or go out of our heads. I'm opting for the former; I just don't know, exactly, how I'm going to do that. It really is just Ghermezi and me against the world. *Akh* …

She knew what I was thinking about, yet didn't make a sound; she didn't need to ask what was playing ping-pong in my head. They were the things on the mind of every strapping sixteen-year-old – unless, of course, you're Babak and have the prettiest bird in Tehran on your arm. I thought about how they were probably going at it, the two of them, while I was sitting up by the mountains drinking beer, watching the night dissolve in ringlets of blue and the voice of Khanum Googoosh beneath a warm yellow glow. Auntie went to the loo, and I took advantage of the intermission to gulp down my beer and crack open a new one, along with a handful of salty pistachios drenched in lemon juice. It was a Thursday night, after all, and I'd have been damned if I was going to sit there and let Arezu and Babak be the only ones having a good time. I wonder if they have pistachios as good as ours over in London. Of course they do – they have everything there.

10

Auntie says the sky is blue wherever we go, but I beg to differ; in Tehran, it's always obscured by a perennial miasma, a hazy pall of soot and exhaust, hanging over the heavens and veiling the brumal peaks of the mountains yonder. Auntie, unlike Mum and Dad, has been around; she's been to places I've only read and heard about in books and songs, like Paris, where she studied to become an artist. I always ask her why she decided to come back to Iran, particularly after the Revolution, and the answer is always the same: she draws in a cool haze of smoke, lets out a heavy sigh, and looks at the flag emblazoned with the Lion and Sun, still sitting proudly on her bookshelf after all these years. 'It's *home*', she says in tones implying her sentiments will be lost on me. 'Home, one's country, wherever it is, is something else.' Perhaps she's right when she says that I don't understand; why would anyone – in my scruffy little sneakers, anyway – want to stay here on this manic dead-end street, in this place where all roads lead to nowhere? What is there going for me here at 'home', in this land Auntie and my parents can't ever bear to leave? I wish, sometimes, that like some other families, we'd packed our bags and gone somewhere nicer, like London, or even sunny Los Angeles (or, 'Tehrangeles', as they call it), where I could do anything I wanted, where I wouldn't dream on my pillow only to be reminded, come dawn, of the pointlessness of it all.

If this is home, then I, for one, don't want it. Everywhere, along with Arezu's haunting eyes and Ferry's voice, in nauseating afternoon shadows and under the sickly skin of the city, I'm hounded by the question once put by a dapper guitar-slinging Bowie: *We live for just these twenty years – do we have to die for the fifty more?* I don't even know why I bother going to school; I should just be plotting my escape instead of sitting here ranting to myself in my bedroom. At elementary school, they told me I'd never get anywhere in life with my attitude, and high school only seems to be confirming things. I spend my days at that cesspool damning the sycophants in the front rows, doodling guitars in every shape and form in the margins of my inky papers, dreaming about Arezu (naturally), and drawing cartoons of my teachers that never fail to reach their desks. If they're going to bring me down, ultimately, I might as well enjoy myself as much as possible in the process. Especially after Arezu entered the scene, my grades went down the toilet; but, supposing I started caring and developed a taste for my teachers' backsides, would it really make a difference? At the end of the day, there's the bloody *konkoor* examination to be taken, the trial by fire that determines who in this life wins, and who loses. They put you up against a horde of the country's most notorious nerds, odious little creatures with checkered shirts tucked in their ill-fitting trousers, to fight for a handful of places. I'll be dead on arrival. That, more or less, means that one year from now, far from my sofa and my rock and roll heroes on the television, I'll be doing my mandatory two years' military service, God knows where. Not having gone to university means it'll be the pits, and I certainly won't have the luxury of being picky. If I'm lucky, I'll get to stay here in Tehran, but if not … I'll have to become inured to life in some sleepy outpost by the Turkish border, or in sweltering Sistan. When you think about it, two years isn't that much in the grand scheme of things; it'll only be a fraction of the time I've already wasted up till now. Bowie says that there's some starman in the sky. That's what I need right now, some starman to grab my hand and take me far, far away from home; and by God, Auntie, I'll never look back. I wonder, though, if I'll even be able to see my shiny saviour through all this smog…

11

It was a quarter to twelve when the rain finally gave us respite. Auntie lay sprawled out on the sofa in a slumber, with an exhausted cigarette still wedged between her spindly fingers, oblivious to all and sundry thanks to Messrs. Walker and Winston. Without disturbing poor Auntie, I called a nearby taxi agency for a ride back home to sleepy Cypress Lane, and also let Mum and Dad know that I'd be home soon. As usual, five minutes became fifteen, the better part of which I spent watching garish macaroni and soap adverts. When the jingle of the intercom gave Auntie a rude awakening, I kissed her smoky cheeks, checked to see if I had any *tomans* left in my pocket, and ambled out onto a mosaic of smooth, wet tiles.

In the rickety white Paykan, ponging with a stench of sweat and tobacco intensified by the moisture of the evening air, the driver was listening to the sparkly sounds of a *santur* overlaid with sombre recitations of mystic verse. He had known from before that he would be driving me down from the idylls of the mountains to blackened Cypress Lane and my pin-ups, and as such, not a word was exchanged between us as he bumped and bounced his way through the undulating back alleys, wet and glowing in the night. Stray cats, whitewashed walls, corner stores, and everywhere, sweeping green branches bathed in droplets. There must have been something in the air, or the music, or a marriage of the two, that brought on a wave of warmth as I rested my head with its sable tresses on those plush blue seats macerated with cigarette burns and scratches. An ineffable calm, a glimmer in the gloom, the absence of motion amidst the tumult. I rolled down the window, simply looking at things, soaking everything in. My city looked more beautiful than ever that night, in hushed hues beneath holes in the sky. I felt like Bryan Ferry in *Avalon*, like Keith Richards, like Ziggy Stardust, as if skinny little me in torn blue jeans and a cherry-red guitar by my side could, against all odds, *rise*. I felt impatient for the morning sun, yet didn't want the night to end. Stretching my arm outside the window, I touched the face of the lucid yellow moon, imagining a band playing on the radio, with rhyming guitars and all, just as they'd said. I imagined then, recalling all the sounds and visions floating around in my head, that I was in London, magical London, so pretty did the world look in my eyes. Nay, it was prettier than London or any other place; it was not the stuff of earth, but Elysium. All the while, a little voice was whispering through the wisps of my hair tossing about in the wind. It told me, softly, that my dreams weren't as silly as I sometimes imagined them to be, and that some way, somehow, everything would be all right in the end. I have never been happier than I was at that moment, sitting in the back seat of a Paykan, watching the world outside whizz past, rolling down the mountains into the heart of Tehran.

12

It was a rock and roll morning – coffee, Keith, and the like. I didn't have to sit through too many Roxette and Bonnie Tyler videos today before they played the Stones on VH1. The moment in that clip, where Mick walks towards the centre of the screen and Keith emerges from its edges, snarling like a total badass and banging away on his old Telecaster with that languid look in his swarthy, wasted eyes … is there anything cooler than that, more flawless? Keef, my hero, the one who tells me that, yes, a little boy with a bright red guitar can change the world and be a hero amongst men. Jamshid's lying through his dirty teeth when he says he doesn't dig him or rock and roll; who wouldn't want to be like Keith? When I ask him who he looks up to, he starts waxing eloquent about some funny-looking Frenchmen long dead. To him, rock and roll is but a puerile pursuit, a plaything of kids who never want to grow up. It's all silly in Jamshid's eyes, but to me, that's exactly the point. I don't ever want to 'grow up', if that means dressing like some fat old accountant and burying my nose in philosophy books, thinking pretty thoughts that get me nowhere and complicating the hell out of what could be an otherwise sweet and simple life. I want to dress like a pirate and wear a skull ring, and bandy around an electric guitar with wild abandon. I'll toss those books aside and walk around like Keef, like rock and roll personified, oozing with decadence and swagger, and no one's going to stop me, honey! Well, perhaps the authorities will, if I get too carried away.

What Jamshid also doesn't understand is that it's not *all* child's play; there is, what I like to call the 'art of Keith', which I've got down pat: the hair, the walk, the kick in the air, the way he strikes a guttural G chord and lets go of his guitar with both sinewy arms. One does not become a rock and roll star overnight, though; it has only been through endless days and nights waiting for my idol to pop up on the flickering television screen, and sultry afternoons cloistered away in my room that I have been able to grasp – and master – the art. The minute the school day is done, I scurry back home to sleepy Cypress Lane, sling my guitar over my shoulder, turn up the volume, and strum along to my Stones tapes and records. I've played Madison Square Garden, El Mocambo, and Altamont, all in my dingy little room: the windows, the threshold between the boys and the crowd; the fluorescent bulb above, the bright lights of the stage; and the black birds hanging on the boughs outside my window, my audience. Always, up in the front row, eyeing me with elation and licking her hot red lips before slipping away into the darkness, is Arezu. Yes, I can get the kids dancing, rock a crowd, and strut about like a Persian popinjay; but what's the use when no one is listening, when no one's around? Notes seep into the walls in a daze, only to tell secrets in the dead of night. I hope the crows, at least, dig the Stones.

* * *

Where, oh where can I find a pair of skinny black trousers and a tight brown blazer in Tehran? I could do with a little variety in the wardrobe department. I'm going for the Keith look, circa 1981. In this city, certain years evoke particular images and memories from a chronicle of embers; to me, however, they bring to mind my records. When I think of 1971, I don't recall the Shah's imperial celebrations, but rather, mouthfuls of brown sugar in the season of the bitch; similarly, 1978 means disco-punk and *Some Girls* more than it does shit hitting the fan and turbaned throngs taking to the streets. And, while the world had waged war on Iran in the early 80s, Keith and co. were knocking back beers in seedy corner bars to the sound of chiming guitars. That, today, is exactly the booze-soaked picture I have dripping before my eyes.

I've tried both the Tajrish Bazaar and the Eskan shopping centre, but to no avail; everything looks the same here, just as the people who buy them look identical to one another: boys with graphic muscle tees and electrified hairdos, girls with bursting lips, painted faces, and more powder than a Colombian drug cartel. If this is what kids are like in the Islamic Republic, it frightens me to think about what they'll morph into if let loose. Cartoon characters they are, the whole lot of them, forever trying to one-up the plastic bimbos and heartthrobs they see singing on their saccharine screens. In this town, nobody wants to be Keith or Freddie; they'd rather be like … oh, I don't even know their names – there are new ones every other week. My pin-ups, though, will never change. I have, however, been going through a strange New Wave phase at the moment, perhaps because of the slew of sappy 80s videos they've been playing all throughout the week on the television. Oddly enough, I've developed a taste for Roxy Music and Spandau Ballet, even if the sweet queasiness they send shooting down my stomach gives me the shits. I bet I can find a suit like Bryan Ferry's lurking somewhere in Dad's closet…

For now, I'll have to simply trade, in my mind, my tattered blue jeans for skinny black ones, and imagine Mirdamad Boulevard to be some leafy street in Kensington (I've heard it's quite nice). It isn't so difficult, really, if you just blur your eyes a bit, walk around with the first two buttons of your shirt undone like you don't give a fuck, and puff away, while the sound of a tight rock outfit crunches in every cranny of your being. Of course, a shot or two of the good stuff on the sly always helps, so long as they don't sniff you out; it'll be curtains for my *kakol* and me, then, if the whip *really* comes down. Imagining is one thing this city has taught me well; I wouldn't have survived this long had I not been able to hear the brash clang of guitars in dead back alleys and trace wooden curves in the clouds. It forces you to imagine, this place, to see things that are here, but aren't, to hear things that are sounding, somewhere else, to feel like Keith Richards in the shadows of a sweltering afternoon, when you're only a skinny little kid in beaten-up sneakers.

13

I couldn't nab any swag, but I did, at least, manage to find Jamshid later that afternoon. He's been a bit off his rocker recently, and I reckon it has something to do with all those books of his; you can never get a hold of him. It's either that he's wrinkling the supple spine of some vanilla-scented tome, or worse, meditating. He says I should try it, that it will help take my mind off of things, help me see things more clearly, get to know myself better, all that jazz. I could, I suppose, use a bit of winding down these days; but no one's ever going to convince me that the sound of the hum in your brain outdoes that of a beer-battered boogie. To each his own, I say; Jamshid gets his rocks off with philosophy, and I with my guitar. That's just Jamshid, though. He's always been that way, and I'll always love the guy for it. Next to him, the bookworm mystic makes me look drop-dead cool.

I've known Jamshid for ages. My dad and his used to count beans together back in the day at the same accounting firm, and we somehow hit it off. He's older than me (although by only two years), as are most of the handful of friends I've had throughout the years. I suppose it's because I've never really dug football, and have never been one for hanging out with the boys; I've failed to see the point. What's the most you can expect? None of them can play the guitar or hold a note, anyway, so it's not as if you can even get a group going with them. With girls, though ... with girls, there's always a sense of excitement, that something could happen; that you could fall in love – and *be* loved – find that other starry-eyed cloud-gazer with whom you could exchange letters scented with perfume and secrets, and sip on gilded draughts to the hot strum of a burning electric guitar. No, I don't want to go where the boys go; I'm looking for a kiss – always have been, always will be, I, who have always been falling in love with nymphs smelling of flowers and sweets.

It all started with my maths tutor, Khanum Esfandiary. What did she expect, coming over to our house with those red lips of hers and waves of long fulsome locks that poured over her shoulders when she undid the ends of her blue *hejab*? That all those 'afarins' and 'ahsants' over scalding hot tea and pastries would suffice to assuage the tumult within? Bah! She broke both my balls and my heart, smug Khanum Esfandiary, with that sultry smile and all those fractions she tossed at me. She did, however, to be fair, ruffle my hair and give me a hug when I gave her a 'cute' poem on her last day as my tormentor. After her was Jinoos, bony little Jinoos with painted toenails and pink trousers, Agha Firooz's daughter who sometimes came to hang out at our place while he tidied it up and scrubbed about. But then again, how could I expect anything good from a girl with such a name? You just know, somehow, that a girl called Jinoos is going to be a bitch, just as all boys with the name Arash turn out to be bastards. All those MazMaz crisps and soda-flavoured pastilles we'd wash down with

ZamZam cola on drowsy Friday mornings – what a waste. I thought she was in love with me too, that she dreamt of the boy in blue jeans on Thursday nights as I did my pretty playmate; but, as it would be wont to do over and over again, my imagination ran wild, and I soon found myself watching Kolah Ghermezi reruns all by myself. Jinoos stopped coming over (or perhaps Agha Firooz stopped bringing her) after I told her I was in love with her and wanted her all to myself. Looking back, perhaps it was all a bit too heavy for a ten-year-old.

There were many more after Jinoos – Mandana, Homa, Goli – but the stories were more or less the same: boy meets girl, boy falls in love with girl without her having the slightest notion, boy freaks girl out by declaring his love after a fortnight. Auntie tells me there's someone for everyone, that my sweetheart is out there, somewhere; but then, I think, why is Auntie alone? Why didn't Auntie ever marry? Maybe right now, while the thick hot sun is setting, slowly, behind the peaks of the Alborz Mountains, the one who will love me is clapping her hands to a rock and roll band somewhere in Soho; she, like me, is alone, and has been looking all over London town for her guitar-slinging lover boy, but just can't seem to find him. Where could he be? Perhaps in a sooty little flat on Cypress Lane, hanging fire and burning away summer days stretching like bubblegum? Could he be a Persian punk-poet with thick eyebrows and wild raven hair? Maybe. Or maybe I'm just imagining things again. Maybe I'll never get out of Tehran, let alone go to London, and only pine away in vain for the girl on the fifth floor who doesn't love me back.

14

I ambled into Khosrow's smoke-strewn café at around six, sweet sixteen and never-been-kissed. Moist with the warmth of the dying afternoon sun on my back, and with a half-burnt Bahman dangling between my stained, slender fingers, I felt like Behrouz Vossoughi looking for a brawl in one of those black-and-white films. I would have looked more badass, I thought, if I'd slung a sheepskin-lined denim jacket over my scrawny shoulders, just like he did in *Kandoo*. Who was I kidding, though? These hands were made for riffing, not rapping. I often think about what would happen if someone were to lay a finger on Arezu – what would I be able to do? We'd be goners, both of us. Babak, though, would be able to hold his own with those arms of his, always bursting at the seams of his tight designer tees. Perhaps Arezu has gone for the right guy, after all. No, I couldn't fight to save my life or anyone else's … but I can play a killer guitar, for what it's worth.

Jamshid hadn't arrived yet. I sat myself down in a corner beneath a black-and-white photograph of Flaubert (according to Jamshid – he's the one who recognises these dudes), lit myself another cigarette, and ordered a cup of French coffee, the bitter kind they always bring with a bit of chocolate on the side. Someone was singing some ballad or other to the sound of an old Spanish guitar on the radio, but you couldn't make out the words (nor did it matter, most probably), so bustling was the place that night. Trying to look busy, I pulled out an old notebook and pen from my trouser pocket and stared at the congeries of things I'd scribbled down in it: love songs, chord progressions, to-do lists, gripes. What I was *really* looking at, though, was the girl in the corner of my eye with the black ringlets pouring from the fringe of her pastel green headscarf. She was the only other person, aside from me, who wasn't with anyone. She was sitting there, sipping on a steaming cup of *chai* and blowing smoke into the faces of the luminaries above her in their cracked, dusty frames, perhaps trying to make out the lyrics of the track in the background. I needed someone – *anyone* – to take Arezu off my mind, and as my eyes darted between her eyes and the curled pages of my notebook, I began to imagine us together. In Khosrow's dingy little café, it didn't seem so remote a possibility. I tried to get her attention, stretching my arms, running a hand through my hair, gazing at her before quickly diverting my gaze back down again – but she wouldn't even look at me. It turned out the girl wasn't as innocent as I'd imagined; while at my wits' end, conjuring new gestures to get her attention from the corner table, her face lit up at the sight of a twenty-something guy with hairy arms and Ray-Bans she called 'Azizam'. So much for that. Why do the ugly boys always win?

I was sitting there, deflated, resting one cheek on a hand and not giving so much as a thought as to how warped my expression looked when I heard Jamshid's deep *salam*. Khosrow came to shoot the shit, as did another from the bar. It was the usual: they never have anything to say to me, whom they only know as the little boy who hangs around Jamshid. I can't, for the life of me, imagine these days and nights without him; he's one of the few boys I don't mind. Like me, he's looking for something more, something better, albeit something very different. Jamshid has always been like the older brother I never had, and even though he digs his *belle-lettres* more than he does the blues, I wouldn't have it any other way; one strung-out rock and roller is more than enough to deal with.

He had just returned from his pal Mani's photography exhibition up north in Velenjak, with a bundle of catalogues and old paperbacks stuffed in the tattered rucksack forever dangling by his side. He had some new ones with him that day, although they were all creased and wrinkled, nonetheless: *The Rose Garden* by Sa'di, a book about the Buddha, and a Persian translation of Gandhi's autobiography. It's all Chinese to me, but it's as if every old yellowed page brings Jamshid closer to some truth, some hidden secret he so desperately seeks. Although he has turned into something of a local sage – a fact that the jungle on his face has no doubt lent further credence to – he's also lost his mind in the process. One day, he thinks he has everything all figured out, that's he got the very stars in his hand, while on another, he sees his philosophies smashed to bits in light of some newfound knowledge or creeping doubts. Apparently the 'five strings, two notes, two fingers, and one asshole' philosophy just doesn't cut it for Jamshid; but, then again, *la vie en Keith* isn't exactly for everyone. Jamshid always says he's on the verge of 'finding it', of what all this madness is all about. I suppose I'm lucky, in the sense that I found my truth long ago in a ten-track record with someone's crotch on it.

I was down that evening, and Jamshid, pondering the mysteries of existence over cups of bitter Turkish coffee, could well see it. 'Yes, it's her', I told him between drags; what else could have been on my mind, if not Arezu? To add to that, I hadn't even able to find Keith's skinny black jeans earlier on. Jamshid told me that desire brings suffering, and that the reason I'm unhappy is that I'm too attached to this world and want things that will never truly satisfy me. What a load of bullshit. If I looked like Keith and could call Arezu mine, I wouldn't smoke away wasted Friday evenings at Khosrow's, looking at pretty girls and their big hairy boyfriends. I just can't be like Sa'di and the Buddha; I'm not content to ramble about in rags, and I don't want to get away from this world – it's only that this damned city that keeps coming down on me, closer and closer, with each bright, burning day. You follow your philosophies, Jamshid, and I'll follow my little heart – live and let live. You're not fooling me, and you're certainly not fooling yourself, either. Just wait until you fall in love again – I'd like to see you with all your books and grandiose ideas then. Yes! That's just what you need to get your wits back: not beer or blunts, but a girl with faraway eyes who'll bring you to your knees.

* * *

There was a party going down that night – coke, leggy girls, and so on – but I wasn't having any of it. Listening to the recondite rubbish spewing out of Jamshid's mouth had exhausted me, and I just wanted, strangely enough, to be alone in my own head, in my own thoughts. The girl with the green *hejab* was still there, along with Cro-Magnon man; I slipped out of Khosrow's, unnoticed and beyond their gaze. Outside, an albino ragamuffin in thick-rimmed spectacles was selling coloured pens, and, on a nearby side street, a friendly bum in a shiny chintz suit had taken it upon himself to play the role of a warden, making something out of nothing. This place sometimes feels like a living, breathing comic strip, so many 'characters' does one witness here simply by walking down its cracked, sun-kissed boulevards. Some, like the albino, are rarities, while others pop up regularly amidst the throng: the plastic doll with bursting lips and devilish brows, the bandaged porcupine in his branded t-shirt, the svelte, devil-may-care heartbreaker in her slim *manteau* and tight blue jeans, the artist-cum-philosopher with his greasy ponytail and frayed flannel shirt. And then, of course, there's me, Asha the Hound, the skinny thing from Cypress Lane with wild black hair and matching kicks. Why go out on the tiles when you can indulge in the theatre of the night?

Bright yellow headlights poked holes in the night sky, while urchins scurried about with melting pink and green goo dripping from their tiny hands and scowling shrouds of black flitted by, sinking into the swarm. I wasn't seeing them, though, or hearing the sound of the city; there, surrounded by those creatures of the night, a din of dirty guitars was burning in my ears, setting me aflame. I felt my sneakers tighten, my heels scorch, and my breathing quicken. It wasn't the hopelessness of the crooner's voice I felt against those warbling notes shimmering in golden tones, but an unspeakable agitation and urgency. *This is not my destiny,* I thought. A thirty-something man with thinning hair was holding the hand of a child while his wife, with tattooed eyebrows stained purple by the sun, ogled the vitrines of boutiques with a snakeskin purse clutched in her hand. The sight almost made me retch *You are everything I loathe, everything I don't want to be,* I wanted to say to the man. I won't let this city drag me down, I won't become like them: I will, I – *must* – find a way out. I was born by the foothills of these mountains looming over the horizon, these tawny gods of stone and ice, in the land of the noble, but, *ey Khoda,* I don't want to waste away here. Not while these hands have life in them yet, while my cherry-red guitar can still howl and get all the kids on their feet; not with the knowledge that over there, in the idyll I watch flickering on the television from Mum and Dad's rococo couch, I can be so much more. Ah, would that my little black sneakers could carry me all the way to London Town right now, where, in some seedy haunt in Soho, with Ghermezi's battered neck in my hands, I could feel like a hero, if only for a moment. Just like David said.

* * *

But my sneakers could barely carry my lanky self home that night, let alone to Soho, so heavily did crazy, beautiful Tehran weigh down on me. Perhaps it was because of what Jamshid had said, or the girl in the green headscarf, or Arezu's eyes, or this soul-destroying boredom, or not finding those black jeans, or watching my rock and roll dreams fizzle out, every day, before my eyes, or … perhaps it was some noxious farrago and the hot, viscid night that did my head in. The two French coffees I'd downed earlier at Khosrow's had me wired, and I would have killed for one of Auntie's German beers then; but alas, there was not a drop of the sweet stuff to savour – only the acrid taste of a pack of Bahmans burned throughout the blazing afternoon, bitter coffee, and fate. No beer, no rock and roll, and no girl. *What am I doing here?* I thought to myself as I played with an empty cigarette carton on the steps of a shopping centre, before being shooed away by a watchman with something seemingly lodged firmly up his backside. I lied and told him I was waiting on a friend, but he probably thought I was out looking for a good time, to pick up some belle or other passing by who'd smash me to bits right there in the pandemonium of Vali-ye Asr Avenue. I hadn't the heart to wander about on the streets, but I didn't feel like going back home, either. As sadistic as it seems, I wanted to stay out all night watching the world around me and those whose lips I could only dream about, feeling low and heavy, as always. I know these streets like the back of my bony hand, but these days, I've been feeling out of place, out of my mind, like a hound with nowhere to go and no one to love, scrounging for hope in sickly smelling alleyways, a stranger in a strange land. No, this ain't my scene.

Drifting away in the night, on clouds of exhaust and gloom, I soon realised I was starving and short on dough; and so, I bid that stage of oddities farewell, making my way through its squalid crushed velvet curtains back to Cypress Lane, hoping that the Stones would at least be on the television.

15

What my parents mistook for cholera, or one of the other freak maladies that thrive in the hotpot of sweat and smog that is the Tehrani summer, has turned out to be a simple case of anxiety and depression. Everything these days gives me the shits: those fuzzy 80s videos with their sickening synthesisers, the unbearable heat, instant coffee, Zoghali burgers, childhood memories, old neighbourhoods, the insidious creep of September and the coming autumn rains, the old paperbacks at the old hotel (and the hotel itself), the pretty girl on the fifth floor and that arsehole … *everything.* On the bright side, I may have discovered the holy grail of laxatives; better out than in, as I always say. I think I've become allergic to the city itself, which may explain why, for the past few days, I've shut myself up in the apartment, only venturing out in the strange world at dusk for cigarettes and soda pop. At first, it was difficult, but I seem to slowly be getting the hang of dozing off for hours on end. Today I managed to wake up at four in the afternoon, leaving only a few hours between a thick, hot sun beating down boyhood vestiges and the languor of the night. At least, when I was younger, I used to look forward to the coming school year, deeming it an end to my summer boredom, and seeing within it the promise of new friends, love interests, and above all, an excuse to get out of the house. Now that, too, only gives me the shits.

My eyes are heavy, my mouth tastes like chalk, and, as the air conditioning isn't working again, I've been writhing here between these sweat-soaked sheets for the past two hours. I don't bother eating much anymore, seeing as anything I ingest soon turns to a melancholic mush, and have developed the strange ability to subsist on coffee crystals, cigarettes, and potato chips alone. Take that, Gandhi. The television doesn't interest me, I don't care to watch Arezu leave the building whenever I catch sight of her blue headscarf from above, and good old Ghermezi has been languishing away in the corner of my room, gathering dust in shafts of light that manage to slip through my satin shades. I hold her, stroke her supple neck with my sticky palms and … nothing happens. If I can't work an electric guitar, what good am I? I won't even be able to call myself a rock and roller, then. My fingertips are softening, slowly, along with my body and soul, rotting away. Does it matter, though? What's the use of an electric guitar that no one will ever hear? I don't know why they even bother selling these things here; but maybe there are more Chris de Burgh fans and schmaltzophiles in this city than I'd like to think.

Perhaps, instead of killing the days between the sheets, I should instead be plotting my escape. How will I ever get out of this apartment, Cypress Lane, Tehran … *this?* Whenever I put pen to paper, my mind goes blank. I know I have to get out – I just don't know *how.* I have no chance in hell of getting into university, don't have a factory to take over from Daddy-o, don't have a passport that can get me anywhere decent, and – worst of all – don't have any money. We're not what you'd call poor, but we aren't rich, either; we've always been stuck somewhere in the middle, never having been dragged down into wretchedness, but never having poked our heads through the echelons up high, either. Soon, I'll have to waste two more years serving time in the army. You know what that means: no guitar, no rock and roll, no Keef on the television, no pretty girls to daydream about, no *point* whatsoever; and, of course, they're going to deprive me of my second-most prized possession, the beautiful black *kakol* resting atop my head, for which I have laboured not little. My hands break out into a sweat just thinking about the menacing buzz of a Moser and its cool, feral jaws eating away at my pride and joy. Why, and for what? To emerge a beaten up, tossed around, sodomised son-of-a-bitch who's just shit a good chunk of his youth down the drain. Well, I suppose if they at least let me keep my *kakol* and take along my guitar with me it wouldn't be *so* bad. It would certainly be more exciting than this.

I could run away. I have thought about it quite often, particularly on these long, scorching days with no one to see and nothing to do. I could pull a Gheysar and flee from the law in style, with the cops hot on my shiny black heels; but Gheysar died in the end, didn't he? Zaer (nay, *Shir Mammad!*) did get away, though, in that little boat of his. Maybe they could smuggle me out, guitar, *kakol* and all. I could then play the refugee card like so many of the others who've run away and spun stories abroad. It'll be just like a scene from one of those Hollywood films with the old, angry judges. *Your Honour, I can't go back to my country – there's no place for a skinny little rock and roller like me over there. They'll shave my kakol and smash my cherry-red guitar to pieces. Please, Your Honour, I beg thee.* It might just work, especially if I write some inflammatory song against the government and warrant a *fatwa* or two. Then, I'll be Asha the Hound, the Persian punk-poet on the run and out of love, with a price on his head and fire in his guitar. It sounds quite romantic, come to think of it; they could even use that as an opener at my gigs. But first, I'll have to get out of here in one piece; timing, after all, is everything. 'Big Behnam', they call him: if anyone can smuggle me and Ghermezi out of here, it's him. But what about the dough? *Akh…*

16

The blasted three-note chime of the intercom. *Ey vay.* I'd forgotten that Uncle Kourosh, his wife Nahid, and that damned Keyvan would be stopping by that afternoon. I'd told Mum to let them know I wasn't here, and had closed the door shut; for all they'll knew, I was out with Jamshid or ogling guitars in the bustle of Jomhuri Avenue. I don't mind Uncle Kourosh and Zan Daei, but I could never stand that little odious wretch of theirs, with his bestial tantrums, nauseating laughter, and vile crudity. The thing literally climbs up walls and can turn a place upside down; and what's even more unnerving, perhaps, is that his parents sit back and take in the whole spectacle, unfazed, as if watching a flower in bloom. *There goes Daddy's boy; yeah, you shit all over their house – show 'em who's boss!* Uncle Kourosh and Nahid say that they're leaving him alone to 'realise his potential'. He'll make a fine beast, I say. What that thing needs isn't space to push the limits of his savage temperament, but a right slap on the back of the neck.

Did I ever mention I don't like kids? True, Keyvan – nay, *Heyvan* – is a breed unto himself, but I can't stand the lot of them altogether. It was the end of Keyvan, in my eyes, when, during one of Mum and Dad's gatherings,

I heard the dull rattle of nickel and steel coming forth from my bedroom. There, to my horror, did I see that execrable mongrel hitting away at my beloved cherry-red guitar with those pudgy hands that had been God knows where. He screamed when I snatched Ghermezi from him, the bastard, drawing the attention of all and sundry – including Uncle Kourosh and Nahid, who censured me from the throng and shouted, 'He's only a kid!' Mum called me cruel, and for the rest of the evening all had to put up with his futile clamouring and wails. He's not a kid – he's an *animal*; but, kid or not, I swore he'd never touch my guitar ever again.

Mum and Dad smile whenever I express my abhorrence at the sound of a little thing screaming itself purple and sending every manner of slime flying into the air, or the sight of tiny urchins running about, marking their territory like pack animals and smearing their filthy little fingers on everything in sight. They say I'll soon eat my words when I have kids of my own, and that until I become a father, I won't understand anything. Can you imagine? *Me,* Asha the Hound, having … *kids?* I'd rather go blind. It's simply not happening – ever. It's not just that I don't like the tiny wretches, but also childhood itself. My way of seeing things, right or wrong, is that when you have kids, you *become* a kid; afternoon naps, the first day of school, the misery of school, the depression of puerile longing and heartache – you have to go through it *all over again.* I can't bear the thought of it; I haven't put sixteen years of melancholy and disillusion behind me for nothing, and I'll be damned if I have to relive them. I never look back – there's nothing there. I don't miss childhood or the 'good old days', as some call them. I'm just waiting for all of this rubbish to end, for the moment when I get on that bright white plane with my howling red guitar in hand, and burn up the past, these wasted days. The future, whatever it may hold, is all I can look towards, the only thing affording promise and solace. I won't look back, I never will – not even in anger.

* * *

I could hear the son-of-a-bitch running around in the living room, the thud of his sneakers on our floral carpets, the smack of his hands sullying the whitewashed walls. Some washed up Tehrangeles has-been was singing on the television, against phony prattle and the clinking of Mum's new teacups with Nasereddin Shah's mustachioed face on them. I should have gone to the loo one last time while I had the chance, but then, it was too late. Out there, Uncle Kourosh was telling Mum about their trip to the Caspian Sea and Keyvan's mathematical ingenuity. His mind, they say, belies his years; that is why, precisely, he has few friends at school. It isn't easy being a child prodigy, the centre of all those jaundiced gazes. *Oh, for fuck's sake. Your son doesn't have many friends because he's a prick.* Keyvan's time in the spotlight soon ended, and they began talking about me. 'Asha? He's fine, busy with things, getting ready to go back to school, you know.' Again, that sickly, sinking feeling, that rumble in the pit of my stomach and all those tingling, stinging digits. They don't know about my dreams, about the pretty girl on the fifth floor who smells of cotton candy, about this soul-destroying ennui, these sleepless nights, and the delirium of these four walls that shrink with each passing day. Asha isn't fine, Mum; he's lost and in love.

To the wee wretch's credit, they all shut up, if only for a moment. I could never stomach the sound of others talking about me in my absence. Keyvan had become livid again, and was pounding his sticky fists on the glass coffee table, making the Pivot of the Universe shake and shudder in his porcelain saucers. '*Shhh,*' they said, in sibilant tones, 'the kid wants to sing!' I could no longer hear the faint voices of the badly permed has-beens on the television, only a cacophony of guttural noises, yelps, and the stomping of feet; it was music, at least, to Uncle Kourosh and Nahid's ears. 'Afarin', I heard Mum say perfunctorily. She, like me, was probably wondering when this farce was going to end, so that she could at least whip something up before Dad came home from the office. The thuds got louder, he was clapping his hands together fervidly, and seemed to be making some sort of barbarian entreaty. 'What do you want, dearest?' asked Nahid. *Oh no,* I thought, *not Ghermezi. Not today, little savage. Listen to Mum – the guitar is in Asha's room, and you can't go in there; the door's closed shut, and he's out. Why aren't you listening, wretch? Is the tongue of men but babble to your barbarian ears?* 'I want his *geeeetar!*' shouted Keyvan. *Ey Khoda, thou alone art my refuge!* I cried within; but my entreaty fell on deaf ears. His footsteps were sounding heavier, and I could almost smell the thing approaching. Damn whoever put together this miserable flat! Damn Uncle Kourosh for not putting a leash on that beast! My door doesn't even have a lock. I knew he'd be in my room in a matter of seconds, catch me red-handed, snatch away my cherry-red guitar with his vile members, and giggle away with glee at his twofold discovery. Son of a *bitch*! He had this hound cornered, with his tail between his legs. *Think, Asha, think!* I whispered to myself. My eyes fell upon the closet and its half-opened door. 'Giddy-up, Ghermezi', I said, turning the rusty key…

17

Keyvan burst into my room, his chopped, infernal giggles having then abated and his eyes glowing deviously in the shards of light piercing through the cream-coloured blinds. Neither I, nor my beloved Ghermezi, were anywhere to be found. 'Come, dearest', they called from afar, but alas, in vain. The creature just wouldn't give up; it was as if he could smell me, standing behind my newly laundered shirts in my closet clutching onto my guitar, goaded on by some savage sense. He smeared his slimy hands on anything he could find, such was his resolve to find the cherry-red guitar that had been rudely wrested from him on that soggy April's eve. Did he need to smear my pin-ups, those heroes resting proudly above my bed? What had Keef ever done to him? He ransacked the place with such alacrity, the wild thing, while out in the living room, Uncle Kourosh and Nahid sipped away sedately, watching their beastly brood push the envelope, and Mum, befuddled, was probably wondering where on earth I was. I damned them all between clenched teeth in that closet, each and every one of them. Didn't Mum know how much I loved my battered cherry-red guitar, that worn and weathered stuff of dreams? Or were confounded politesse and decorum in the presence of her guests – and, more importantly, her elder brother – of more importance?

Not the closet, I thought, invoking the name of all that was holy and hurling down curses on the fiend at once; but oh, my time had come, right here in this dingy room on Cypress Lane, and nothing could save me – not my rock and roll dreams, not the night in Niavaran, not the Stones on VH1. I espied him through the slit between my closet doors, and though he didn't return my gaze, he knew, by process of elimination, that this was the only possible place I could be. The louse let out a dumb chuckle – his own way, then, of saying 'fuck you' – before slowly prying open the closet door to find both me and my guitar caught in the act. Though having been discovered, I still clung onto the hope that he might not, perhaps, betray my secret, and instead, scamper on back to watch Andy on the television. Our eyes met, and he just stood there, looking at me with that odious smile of his; he knew he had me cornered and in those besmirched paws of his, and wanted to relish every second of his triumph over the boy who had once prised away from him the ruddy thing with the silver strings. It wasn't too long, though, before he broke his silence; he couldn't contain his excitement. 'Maman! Maman! I've found him!' came the ejaculation, after which Mum, Nahid, and Uncle Khosrow came walking, slowly, into my room. There was no use in trying to do anything at that point; the kid had won. There I stood, a hapless little hound, in my blue jeans and black kicks, clutching Ghermezi to my breast in two sweaty palms. 'I want the *geeeetar*', the thing had the nerve to say again, as if I hadn't been mortified enough. For some reason, in spite of the circumstances, I remembered Jamshid, as they stared at me in disbelief, Mum with her finger pressed to her lip like in those flowery miniatures of Khosrow and Shirin. Jamshid would have only laughed, had he been in my tattered Converse sneakers then, thinking that he might as well make the best of it. 'What do you want me to do? Cry?' he'd often ask me, before flashing his tea-stained teeth.

So I laughed. The rest of the sultry afternoon, exacerbated by rounds of scalding hot *chai* in Mum's Qajar teacups and the whinnies of the Californian Neanderthals on the television, passed by in a blur.

That evening, I couldn't help but grin as I recalled the episode, halfheartedly watching Boy George in a swimming pool and chewing on cola-flavoured pastilles. I hated Keyvan more than ever, though, and wasn't feeling too fond of Uncle Kourosh and Nahid, either. I knew things with them would never be the same, and that every time they saw me, they'd be sure to picture me huddled in that closet with the guitar I wouldn't let their kid play. At least he didn't smear his dirty fingers over it; I would have done the beast's head in right then and there. There are two things in this life I won't let anyone touch: my hair, and my guitar. I'll be damned if anyone's going to lay a finger on my precious *kakol* or Ghermezi's sparkly strands. But what am I even doing sitting here thinking about such trifling things? To hell with Keyvan and Uncle Kourosh, *mehmoonis,* idle chatter over tea, and the synthetic sounds of sunny Tehrangeles. Is it selfish to think I've been destined for better things? Is it ungrateful of me to be discontent here on sleepy Cypress

Lane, dressing up like rock stars in front of my mirror and waiting for the Stones to come on VH1? It could be worse, I suppose; but every night, when I rest my swarthy locks on my cool pillow, a little voice down inside tells me that this is not the life I'm supposed to be living. No, this isn't it.

18

I'm beginning to see myself in flowers. I don't know whether it's because I've been staring at the sooty boughs of the towering trees outside on Cypress Lane, or if it has anything to do with that little musty book of Jamshid's still lying around. So numb has my mind become from this vapidity that I've even taken to reading it from time to time. Where does Jamshid get these things from? Could he have discovered my haunt? Perhaps he found it among those other old odds and sods from fizzled out decades rotting away, ever waiting, solemnly, to be caressed, to see again the sun. Maybe, but that's not the only place to stumble upon relics here. The whole place is a relic itself, a breathing, beating museum, a palimpsest of concrete, exhaust, and dreams. Forgotten hours and sighs endure yet on the streets of this city, in dark alleyways, under blankets of dust, in blackened holes in the wall and forlorn crannies, in hot, fading rooms that have slipped through the silken sheet of time. Everything is here, as real and palpable as ever – if only you feel for it. The odd vestigial note echoes from the burnt-out club on the street corner, laughter rings down the undulating halls of the crumbling hotels when no one's listening, the scent of lost beloveds emanates from baked walls of clay and the stained seats of moribund Paykans, telling tales of what was once, and what will never again be. Under the sordid skin of the city is a veiled romanticism, cloaked before unseeing eyes, soaking through Tehran's every pore. It is this splendour swathed in slumber that I have always loved, those things gone but still here, secrets shrouded by smoke, the living past.

> *This jug was once a downcast lover, like me,*
> *Entangled in the locks of a fair beauty.*
> *This handle you see, which on its neck rests,*
> *Is a hand that once a beloved's neck caressed.*
> – Omar Khayyam

There is a room down a dusty, forlorn corridor, beside a florist in the old Hyatt hotel. Somehow, the post-Revolution 'Azadi' just hasn't caught on amongst us, as has been the case with many other such names. In this city where the past lives and speaks, the streets have two names – sometimes more – as if, while the sun beats down on their cracked faces, they whisper, 'Lest we forget'. I know them as Vali-ye Asr and Shariati, but to Mum and Dad, they'll always be Pahlavi and the Jadeh Ghadim, the Old Road. Sometimes, even buildings have two numbers, one old, and one new. You have to know both names and numbers, and are always suspended in some liminal state between the past and the present, at once in both, yet never in either of them alone. One gets used to it, like anything else after a while, I suppose.

In that room, barely large enough for two people to move about in, sits a weary man with sweat patches on his baggy beige buttoned-up shirt. We never exchange many words, yet know each other well, and I always get the feeling that some unspoken pact exists between us. His eyes tell me that he knows his secret is not unknown to me, and mine give him the assurance that it is safe. Sitting there before his sundry wares, he offers them for sale, yet doesn't want to see them go; for they are not just any old curios, but mementos of a bygone age, gilded with dust and unmarred by the vicissitudes of time. Seldom is a soul seen wending throughout the sombre void of the corridor, let alone the old man's shop, lying at the end in a state of perpetual preservation in glass and cellophane. That, perhaps, is what adds to its allure in my eyes; when I walk in and see those yellowed English paperback novels untouched on the squeaky rotating rack (always in the same position in which I last left it), I feel a sense of possession, as if it's mine, and mine alone. Just as I have *my* guitar and *my* song, so do I have my own special places, of which that old curio shop is one. I haven't told anyone about it – not even Jamshid. I wouldn't betray the old man's eyes, or our little secret, for anything.

There, beneath the soft yellow glow of the lights above, and the flickering hues of the little television in the corner silently replaying last night's football behind a spate of dots and scratches, I am alone with my vanilla-scented remnants of a life I never knew, of worlds as marvellous as they are strange. I've looked at those dusty novels with creamy pages and virgin spines in the island tongue a hundred times, and can look at them a hundred more. I almost forget Arezu and her faraway eyes as my fingers, moist with sweat, turn black flipping through them and I relish their sweet aromas wafting from within. These candied tomes have been, along with my rock and roll records and the videos on the television, my summer education. Packed like sardines into the tiny revolving bookcase are Inspector Ghote crime novels, tawdry romances and science fiction novels with robots and men with guns on them, and the creepy-looking *Secret Life of Plants,* amongst others. Along with *Pop, Rock, and Soul* with Keef and the butterfly on the cover, I also picked up *I Couldn't Smoke the Grass on My Father's Lawn* by Charlie Chaplin's son the other week, though I have yet to read it. *Pot, Girls, and Swingers in London's Ultra-Mod Set*: the description alone is music to my ears. Pot, girls, and swingers in a government-owned hotel in the heart of Tehran? It's our little secret.

Also collecting dust in the time machine of the jaded old man with his burly, drooping moustache are 70s travel guides to Iran in all sorts of languages – English, French, German – still wrapped in cellophane, various editions of Morier's *The Adventures of Hajji Baba of Ispahan*, black-and-white Qajar-era photographs by Antoin Sevruguin, ornate, multiple-language editions of the *Divan* of Hafez, and other colourful tokens from halcyon days reduced to blurs and celluloid: old bottles of cologne, obsolete electronics, postcards, all conspicuously pre-1979. It is always, however, that rickety bookrack that draws me in, and one book in particular that I often flip through and smell, but have never read; I'll buy it, one of these days, after I finish the two I've just bought, and the one Jamshid's lent me. On the cover is a man with curly hair and deep brown eyes, not unlike mine, and a blonde woman in a billowing dress with a sort of phantom presence. *Do You*

Remember England? All I can remember is the woman in red with flowers in the wood, singing about some guy called Heathcliff. What other images do I have, except for the fuzzy ones flickering on the television and through my head? My England is one of verdant moors, dandies in juke joints, and wet streets illumed by gaslights. It is there, in the warbling expanses of my mind, in words unsaid, in the howls of battered cherry-red guitars; and Paradise lies beyond the jagged, jutting mountains poking holes in the sky, beyond these black clouds, beyond the diaphanous veil of destiny. I will remember England, one day.

* * *

The very thought of the bookstore is giving me the shits as I lie here, digging my tingling heels into the floral sprays of the sofa in our living room, waiting for Jamshid to call back, waiting for the Stones to come on the television, waiting, always, for something to happen. I can feel again that peculiar, sweet sickness with echoes in those ethereal, quivering chords. Though it's a bit heavy on my bowels, I have almost developed a fondness for it, as I have for Roxy Music, in a strange, masochistic kind of way; I actually miss them, though I'd much rather see Keef and co. I can't quite put my finger on what exactly draws me to that old bookstore, besides those sweet-smelling pages and the thought of having a 'secret' place. Walking down the shadows of that empty corridor awash in the neon lights of dirty signs, I feel the breath of spirits, whose shoulders brush against my raggedy blazer with sleeves browned by sweat and the sun. It is more the place of the dead than the living, a sort of necropolis of the lingering thoughts of yesteryear, fading, cracked, and burned, all but forgotten. Sometimes, the old man isn't even there, but in the back somewhere, leaving me all alone with those musty mementos. There is a sadness to the place, imparting to one the feeling of being some sort of spectator of a dying spectacle. Pregnant with the air of death and decay, one wonders what will happen to all these odds and sods when the old man breathes his last. Who will read about those creepy-looking plants or remember England, then? More than anything, I am overcome by an overwhelming sense of loneliness; I am always the only one there, often wondering if I am the sole soul who can see any beauty in the place, however bittersweet it may be. I abhor this loneliness, this boredom of mine; yet, I seemingly look for it, in ghostly corridors, forgotten bookstores, and the winding back-alleys of Niavaran. A romantic pursuit, perhaps? I find myself becoming more and more like Jamshid, seeking things in the solitude of his flat, with books and blunts as friends, lighting up and seldom returning to the worries of the world below.

19

Roxette, again: too much melancholy for one lazy summer afternoon. I think I'm going to be sick. From outside comes the banter of the drudges with sunburnt faces and pastel bandanas, and the caw of a black crow. Seen from the side, it almost looks like me, with its angular beak and raven tufts. Today, I can see no beauty in Tehran, which looks particularly ugly. Obscuring the haughty Alborz Mountains in the distance, dotted by bright little lights and covered with cowls of snow, is a noxious haze looming on the horizon. Below the blemished blue sky is a sea of rusty old satellite dishes and sea-green coolers frying in batters of bird shit upon lifeless grey masses streaked with blacks and whites. The street is unusually quiet today, devoid of even the wails of the minstrel in the greasy polo shirt who plays *King of Hearts* on his dirty red accordion while crumpled green bills float down onto Cypress Lane. I only espy through the iron lattices and torn tarpaulins blue and black headscarves here and there, and only hear the scant, garbled words of gamins on their way back from the local bakery or greengrocer, uttered in hot breaths. Through the yellowed walls are coming the dulled vibrations of a *setar* from the flat next door, and somewhere, in the distance, a cicada is sounding the clarion call of summer, of sweltering afternoons, languor, and teenage melancholy; and all, at only one in the afternoon. Give me a beer, give me the Stones, *get me out of here*.

Sipping on viscous instant coffee in a stained white mug, I saw her standing outside the apartment door earlier today, pushing her chestnut tresses back into the recesses of her blue *hejab* beneath the beating August sun. A few white Paykans, differentiated only by the plastic slogans stickered onto their rear windows and their battle-scars, whizzed by in the opposite direction on the one-way street, leaving behind plumes of smoke in their wake. She was waiting, and I knew well for which lucky bastard. Coolly reclining against the iron door marred by rusty patches and little black fingerprints, she took out her bright red lipstick and a little pocket mirror, dolling herself up before an audience of crows and labourers staring at her through those piercing eyes of theirs, looking at what both their hands and mine would never be able to reach. Watching her from up in our living room, with my bony elbows digging into the windowsill, my insides turning to jelly, and my mouth reeking of Nescafé, was like a kind of slow death, intensified by the melodrama of Spandau Ballet on the television. I hoped, as the sun burned through the windows, that she might recall in her waiting the lanky boy on the fourth floor with his *kakol* and his guitar that matched the colour of her lips, and turn around to see, behind fried lattices and a covey of workers, he who loves only rock and roll and her. But she didn't; Babak didn't give her the chance. No sooner had I begun daydreaming again than another Paykan rolled into Cypress Lane, this time a taxicab that stopped before our apartment building;

and Arezu, smiling and adjusting her headscarf again, jumped in the back seat with Babak, leaving me high and dry, stuck in 1983.

Who am I kidding, thinking I'll forget about Arezu if I find someone else? The only reason I ever bothered to put on airs for the girl in the green headscarf at Khosrow's was because she sort of looked like Arezu; even the make-believe girl in the Soho club looks like her. Damn her and those eyes, following me like shadows in the sun, watching me, always, in the classroom, in forsaken alleys, in the thick of dreams. Arezu, with her white neck smelling of cotton candy and cherry-red lips, has become, in my mind, the prototype, the ideal of beauty, to which I can but compare all else. I've been eternally cursed to wander the streets of Tehran and the rivers of sleep in pursuit of those faraway eyes – the kind Mick and Keith sang about in that video I'd never seen before the other week – which seem to recede further and further into the distance, beyond dreams, beyond the mountains, beyond the smoggy skyline of Tehran. The thought of September being only a few weeks away and having to see Babak every day at school is enough to make me retch. How am I ever going to get through this year? I'm just sitting here, a lonely schoolboy on a hot summer morning, waiting to be buried alive.

* * *

It was nearly four in the afternoon when I awoke, flat on my face beside a cool, dark patch of saliva. The labourers were still pounding away on the scaffolding outside, exchanging jagged words with urgency, the crows were still cawing, and I still felt like a proper mess. Summer, too, is a ruse of our teachers, who won't even leave us alone when all's been said and done. They know we'll go out of our heads and become so desperate that even school will appear in our scorched eyes like some *fata morgana,* some paradise lost. Or, maybe it's just me; if I were in Babak's squeaky white trainers, I'd never want August and its long viscid nights to end, ever.

Thank you, God, for the Rolling Stones. Occasionally, on such sickly afternoons, down and out in the nightmare of this flat, I put a record on my little stereo and my hands behind my head, and stare at my pin-ups printed from the all-but-worthless Internet, and the void of my ceiling. I sometimes imagine myself on a stage somewhere with my cherry-red guitar, while at others, think of nothing at all. I usually skip straight to the third track on the Stones album Manuch found me at the start of summer, which has come, in an otherworldly sort of way, to define these two sweltering months: a soundtrack of boredom, yearning, fear, endless waiting, and the shits. Everything these days is seen and felt through warbles, wah-wahs, and cascading keys; but, come September, the music will end, along with these days of fire and ash. In their stead will come new notes, new songs of hope and despair, which I'll play ad nauseam in my head and on my battered guitar, and which will give new meaning to the decay of autumn and the wintry winds. This record, with its haunting yellow sleeve, has turned my blues a lighter hue; but I will, in all likelihood, never be able to listen to it again, without feeling my legs buckle beneath me and these four walls come crashing down. Yea, as August comes to an end, so will these strange, beautiful melodies.

I wish I could be like the pin-up on my bedroom wall, like the badass who pops up in between those slushy 80s videos brandishing his guitar and smoke-stained grin. He doesn't have any teachers breaking his balls or any Babaks snagging his birds. He can get any girl he wants. He's the leader of the greatest rock and roll band in the world, lives in London (probably around Soho), and has as much beer as he wants without having to answer to anyone or feel the crack of a whip. He doesn't have to worry about the university entrance exam, the army, or any of that other rubbish beating around in the back of my head. He isn't stuck in some dead-end street in a dead-end city with a shite passport. He doesn't have to worry about *anything* other than strumming that butterscotch blonde beauty of his. Oh, if I could only be just like Mister Keith Richards…

20

The workers had all gone, having jumped in the back of the shattered blue pickup truck that bumps and grinds onto sleepy Cypress Lane every evening, when Sol's roseate hues slip, ever slowly, through dusk's inky fingers. Mum and Dad came home at around seven in the afternoon, one after the other, only to doff sweaty clothes sticking to limbs wearied by deadlock and the monotony of the working day, doll themselves up, and head out again into the delirium of the world outside these windows to spend the night sipping whisky over little white lies at Firouzeh's. They thought, after all those fuzzy videos of the past rent by jagged streaks of green and purple, all those never-ending candied pages in alien tongues, and all those insidious thoughts seeping through my satin curtains in the glow of the afternoon sun at its most menacing, that I'd only be too eager to get out of the flat for a bit of fresh air and 'fun', as they called it; but you don't leave one shithole only to crawl into another. I preferred my moist sheets and the soft whirr of the air conditioner with the red winking face to playing the role of a hanger-on with Mum and Dad and their friends, feeling like a child, while watching fat old Firouzeh Khanum pass around a blue-labelled bottle of booze and hint with her tattooed eyebrows at my ever-brimming glass, urging me to have another 'dee-reenk'. And I knew, as always, that there would be some spotty kid there whose mum, teetering around in high heels with her big arse bursting out of a tight black miniskirt, would tell him to go and talk to 'that boy' about football and cars. No, I didn't want to go there – not even for Johnnie.

Mum and Dad say they're worried about me. I don't get out enough, I don't have any 'normal' interests, I don't like things other kids my age are into, and I don't care for anyone's company except Jamshid's. I don't like talking about the future with them, or about anything, for that matter. What is there to talk about, anyway? Songs will remain unsung, secrets locked up tight within my bony breast. Mum and Dad wouldn't understand, and Jamshid, the only person I used to be able to talk about these sorts of things with, has morphed into some sort of dervish who only gives fortune cookie answers through his tousled, oily beard. I don't blame them, though; I'm worried too, more than anyone else. Jamshid once told me that, in his search for truth, during a time when his world turned on its head and left his spinning, he'd sometimes find himself in a strange threshold. His mind was awake, but his body, asleep; he could think, but not move, rooted to his bed, as if paralysed – or so he said. I, too, have found myself caught in this liminal state, suspended between motion and inertia. I'd be luckier, perhaps, were I like some of the other kids; they're already dead, but they don't know it. My dilemma is that I *do*; light pokes through the dark veil of death, but what to do? The voices in my head tell me to run, while my little black kicks feel like dull balls of lead. They beckon me to faraway lands blanketed in fog, while my hands remain pinioned in faded pink sheets sullied with night sweats and speckles of lust. I lie under cool, smarting draughts, gazing at a white void above, only able to drown in fear and make out shapes and faces in the prickly moulding of my bedroom ceiling.

They left reluctantly, shaking their heads and softly muttering in confusion. Alone, again. Behnam, one of my classmates, called, but I didn't pick up the phone. I knew he only wanted me to loiter about Shahrak-e Gharb with his stray dog buddies, who often went there to pass numbers to belles in blue jeans glittering against those yellow bricks in the night. A hound I may be, but that has never been my scene. That evening, while cool zephyrs rushed through my window, bringing a promise of rain and cleansing, I missed Arezu more than ever. I wanted her, despised her, damned her, in the sallow shades cast by a bulb's last breaths. Images of her in the elevator and on the street corner flickered between those of her and Babak, until thoughts of the two, together, with heavy breaths, obscured all others. Again, I found myself helpless, yet urged on by voices ineffable and guttural swirls to reach out, with white arms stretched out wide, for something that could never be. Again, I tried to evade the gaze of those faraway eyes, but to no avail. I remembered the sylvan phantom named Cathy, the girl with the green headscarf, the Voice of America anchorwoman, random characters from the street and the satellite, all of whom merged into a long, curvy nose and soft ears poking out of chestnut cataracts and cerulean folds, a haunting, damning, Elysian vision of desire and death.

But there was life in me yet. After rousing myself from

the abyss of an idle mind, I resolved to drink as much as I could, to rock and roll as loudly as I could. Dinner consisted of mixed nuts and vodka, courtesy of the man on the motorbike, the bearer of good tidings. The half moon looked down on me from beneath its sable cowl, and in its pockmarked face, I saw the starman, the saviour of the night sky. Out of an unwonted prurience, I flicked past the call girls twirling curled cords around their painted fingers in the steamy 600s, but, seeing as I lay exposed before the rows of yellow patches outside, let go of the randy thoughts slithering downwards, and instead kicked back with my pistachios, rock and roll videos on VH1, and a bottle of booze.

From behind black sunglasses, beating away on a black Fender guitar, a skinny woman named Patti Smith was singing about mashed potatoes and alligators. We have the same hair, more or less, and the same nose, and I think she, too, likes Mr. Richards. Arezu sort of has a Patti Smith thing going on as well, which is why she's so cool. She rarely puts on any makeup, and her virgin nose, with all its glorious twists, bumps, and edges, has yet to go under the surgeon's icy blade. The girls of this city should take their cues from Patti and Arezu rather than the bouncing bimbos on the other channels and the film posters throughout town. Keith Richards for President, I say; he's the man who can sort us all out, who can get this town reeling and rocking again. A film came out this year called *Tehran Has No More Pomegranates*. My fear is that one day, they'll be saying this city has no more big noses. Nobody's laying a finger on mine – or my prized *kakol* for that matter – and if Arezu ever gets it in her pretty head to solve any 'breathing complications' (as everyone claims they have), there'll be hell to pay. She can break my heart, that girl, but not that nose – and what a nose it is!

The vodka kept pouring, the guitars kept roaring; I, Asha the Hound, the Spider from Pars, howled at the moon, out of my head, and pulled moves atop faded woven flowers. From the neighbours' flat next door came dulled fragments of laughter, muffled claps and cheers, and the sounds of synthesisers aplenty. *This little schoolboy can have a good time, too,* I thought, as my head spun around and I cracked pistachio shells between my spindly fingers; and so, after taking a hearty, burning swig of the good stuff, I raided Mum's closet and dressed myself up to the nines, leaving no stone unturned. I played it by ear: a crushed velvet scarf became a headband, a pashmina served as a cape, and little old *giveh* slippers added the finishing touch. With a bit of kohl and rouge, tastefully applied, I emerged from Mum and Dad's bedroom as some sort of Persian pirate, my veins hot with liquor and love, and my belly full of fire. Think Keith Richards meets Fat'h Ali Shah; his gloriously bearded majesty would have been proud of that rocking ragamuffin, no doubt. The reverberations from behind the thin white walls echoed louder and louder, and so, not wanting to let those pretty things next door one-up me, I cranked up the volume of the television, just as Ziggy and the electric angel leapt onto the screen.

Shrouded in a halo of deep red, he told me I wasn't alone, and I wanted to believe him. I wanted to be there, in the steamy hot pit of the Hammersmith Odeon, with paint running down my face and tears in my eyes as the starman bade this whirling blue ball farewell, clawing at my cheeks, heady with the fumes of forbidden faunae and grinding, bright guitars shining in hot pools of light, lost in a crowd and a world unto myself, always reaching out towards the crimson aura in the distance, trying to better see the man, to touch him, feel him. 'Give me your hands!' he cried, as the longhaired angel's guitar, doused in vitriol, waxed louder and nastier, and the band played on. Sitting on my bony knees, intoxicated, my being in overdrive, transfixed by those sounds and visions streaming through the television unhindered by little dots of black and white and purple screams, I gave them to him. I smeared my slender hands, then puffy and wet with elation and coloured with strains of Mum's makeup, all over the screen, unfazed by myself, by the gilded lozenges of light outside and watching eyes, by Khanum Bahrami downstairs heaping curses upon my raven head and those of my ancestors. For a rare moment, there were no slushy, squeamish feelings in my stomach, no stinging boyhood memories and fears, no breaths, hot, heavy, and empty of hope – nothing but an ineffable lightness and release, a sense of weightlessness, of emptiness. I knew no god but Ziggy, then, no creed but the song of a burning hot cherry-red guitar dripping with teenage sweat and the blood of the daughter of the vine. My prophets dressed in glitter and drag; around their heads burned halos of white light, and they danced, without their feet ever touching the ground, surrounded by spectres with blackened eyes and red leather boots.

I was Ziggy, bathed in red. I was the electric angel. I was the bright guitar, the pools of light. I was the television and the room, the Hound and the Spider, the flowers outside my window, the awl-eyed drudges in their blue pickup truck. All things had their beginning and end in me.

* * *

I don't know for how long I lay there, in paisley and velvet, on the sun-kissed sprays of the Kashani carpet, surrounded by pistachio shells; Ziggy and the vodka had both done a number on my head. Marc Bolan remained frozen on the television screen, with his mouth wide open and in big white shoes, his body cut in half by a strident bright green shard that made the most awful squeals and popping noises. Mum and Dad hadn't come home yet, and no more could I hear the subdued laughs, claps, and flanging southern melodies from the flat next door. In their stead were shrieks, jeers, and the heavy thud of boots. The men in green had struck again. Could it have been Khanum Bahrami who ratted on them? Who knows. Frenetically, I turned off the television, cleaned up the living room, and carefully stowed away Dad's bottle of Smirnoff in its usual hiding place beneath the kitchen sink. I washed the smudged makeup from my face, stuffed away Mum's clothes back in her closet, and, like a thief in the night, stole away beneath my pink sheets, trying to make out what was happening next door. As I lay in bed, upright with an ear pressed to the wall, a black shadow flitted by, outside the window in the corner of my eye, down behind the boughs, followed by a loud crack and a deafening chorus of screams.

und
21

Red dots, peppered on the hot, dusty pavement outside on sleepy Cypress Lane, still turn a deep, brilliant crimson beneath the revelation of the afternoon sun. The papers under the bricks at the little stall at the end of the street say he topped himself, but everyone (at least I and the people upstairs) knows what *really* happened. Trying to evade the menacing men in green, the blue-eyed heartbreaker – the kind you see on movie posters and the cloying covers of crossword puzzles – tore himself away from the tumult on the eight floor and dashed upwards, towards the roof. But the bird had no wings, his torn red Converse sneakers couldn't carry him to the building beyond as they taunted him and yelled from behind, 'Ist!' Flailing his arms, tearing at the sky, as if to hang onto the canopy of little bright lights overhead, he fell. Dead, on a dead-end street.

I couldn't sleep a wink last night, as I clutched onto my sticky rouge-smeared sheets in sweaty fists trying to make sense of it all, my head booming from the booze and a thousand flurrying thoughts. Light soaked through black holes in the blocks of grey across the street, as neighbours, curious to know what had happened on the otherwise dull side-street, opened their windows to gaze down below at the tangled bustle of confusion and hysteria. I couldn't bear to look again at the crumpled mass shrouded in white; only one sentence echoed in my mind while my eyes flickered back and forth between the white void of the ceiling and the knowing boughs outside: *It could have been me.* I felt the same way I do whenever I pass by those harrowing martyr murals in the city, with the faded faces of children surrounded by tulips and slogans. They don't give me the shits – they give me the *chills*. The Hounds could have been playing an underground gig, somewhere in the squalid creases of the city, the kids tapping their feet and clapping their hands to the filthy barks of my battered cherry-red guitar and the boys in the band. Some bastard could have tipped off the police, and they'd have come, those men in green with the long, funny hats, to smash my beloved Ghermezi and drag me by my soon-to-be-shorn *kakol* all the way to the slammer. Maybe I would have endured the trial; or, maybe, like the wingless bird, would have tried to make a run for it, guided by stars, only to end up a lifeless jumble of blue jeans, bones, and black kicks, crowned in sable and betrayed by the night.

I was awake when Mum and Dad came home around midnight from Firouzeh's, but I feigned sleep, pulling my thick, patterned blanket over my head to appear from afar as but a little black tuft. I could hear their worried, whisky-doused whispers in the living room: 'Alas. Strange. *What a waste.*' I didn't feel like talking then, though; I was down enough as it was, and even decided that I'd pretend the next morning as if I didn't know anything. I'd let them do the talking, and just look at them, wide-eyed. I was relieved when they closed my bedroom door to avoid 'waking' me up, although I felt an added pang of terror when I heard Mum ask Dad from the bathroom if he'd seen her lipstick. I'd left it in my trouser pocket, and forgotten to put it back. But it was worth it, I thought, as I fought back an oncoming grin and bit on my pillow's edge, looking proper glam and all.

With my face buried in hot, boozy breaths, listening to the dying sounds outside and Mum and Dad's scratchy footsteps, I felt smaller and more helpless than ever before. How, I thought, would I ever get to England? It then seemed further beyond the solemn-standing mountains than usual, shrouded in soot and gloom, as strange and unfathomable as the stories in our schoolbooks. If only I were as content with things as Jamshid; but I'm not, I *can't* be. For how much longer can I dress up in Mum's clothes, get piss drunk, and wriggle my bony arse around to the blurry pictures of my heroes on the television, imagining myself beside them under those coloured lights, with those shining guitars, with white puffs of heaven beneath our feet? *Khodaya,* don't let me die here, dancing in the dark, behind closed doors and curtains, away from damning eyes and the mean old sun on sleepy Cypress Lane. We were destined for better things, we dirty-sweet children of the moon, for higher climes. Our blood may not run any more ruddy, but it was meant to be spilled on silver strings and screens, mingled with cheap red wine and ash, not on dark and lonely alleyways in the dead of night.

22

We'll be having *tahchin* for lunch today; I can smell those saffron notes seeping beneath the door from the kitchen, where Mum is busy cracking eggs and stirring away. Dad, as usual, is reading the papers over tea in a thin-waisted glass and cigarettes, occasionally lifting his eyes from the pages of *Iran* and *Shargh* to watch the banality of the Channel Two news, with its nerve-racking jingle that always gets cut off before it has a chance to end. I've only left my room once, for the essentialsinstant coffee and biscuits – and otherwise, have spent the morning caged in my bedroom and the confines of my little head, still reeling with a thousand thoughts, big and small, menacing and benign. I don't know what to do with myself today, as usual. It's strange: I spend the whole week in anticipation waiting for Friday to come along, with some unfathomable hope; yet, when it finally rolls along, I find myself at my wits' end. It must be something wired in me, a vestige of childhood days, when Friday meant escape, an end to the drudgery of the infernal school week, a chance to catch my breath before Saturday would kick me in the arse again. What am I waiting for now, though? School or no school, it doesn't make a difference; there's still nothing to do here, at least for me.

Again, the *tat-tat-tat* of Mum's long wooden spoon on the edge of the pot, again the Channel Two chimes and the sound of the man with the phony, booming voice advertising macaroni brands, laundry detergent, and microwaves. He must be a millionaire, that guy who does all those adverts; his voice is everywhere, always urging, imploring, and duping people into buying some sort of rubbish. Why am I even thinking about him, though? Am I *that* pathetic, that while the other kids are out and about, loitering in the streets, having hamburgers, and passing numbers to coveys of sultry girls in dark sunglasses, I'm here listening to what's going on in the living room? I don't know what the Rats have against Monday; it's just another day. Oh, how I hate Fridays. At least during the other days Mum and Dad are out working, and I have the whole flat to myself to brood and be miserable in. Now, I can't even do that; I can either try, somehow, to dig the state television garbage, sit here and wait until Mum calls out, 'Asha, lunch is ready!' or lie to my parents and tell them that Behnam has just sent a text, and that I'm going out for junk food with the boys. But I just don't feel like doing anything today; I don't feel *anything,* period.

Some days I feel so ... *old*. Jamshid often laughs and says that, in many ways, I'm an old man trapped in a sixteen-year-old boy's body; according to him, I'll make an 'interesting' geriatric. He's right, I suppose: I'm angry, grumpy, and disillusioned, and like old things nobody else I know does. But today, as on other summer days, I feel old in a different way. I'm not angry with anyone or thing, but rather, feel like I've had the life sucked out of me. I feel nothing but an overwhelming sense of weariness, both in my mind and in my limbs. I've been thinking so much about things, daydreaming and damning to such lengths that my brain actually hurts, as if it's slowly frying. My arms, legs, and back smart like hell, and my body is one bony, tangled knot. Today, I don't care about Mum's *tahchin,* my rock and roll records, or even Ghermezi, sitting there in the corner beneath my pin-ups, her corroded strings shining in the sunlight. I know there's a whole world out there, a whole universe waiting for me, for Asha the Hound and his battered cherry-red guitar, but I can't even rouse myself from these pillows and sheets. Time seems to be passing me by with every dull and empty day, and all I can do is sit and stare outside my window, watching the blinding ball in the sky sink into the shadows of the night, only to emerge again burning more than ever. What's worse, perhaps, is that I'm slowly getting used to this, watching these 'golden years' (as all the elders call them) be reduced to cinders. Maybe that's why they're like that, those fat, bald men in clothes two sizes too large for them, walking behind their wives and mother-in-laws in the park, while their kids gorge on ice-cream and stick their fingers up their noses; maybe they too are tired, and have simply gotten used to this deathly inertia. Dress up for whom? Get excited for what? Mick and Keith aren't old – *those* people are. No, they're already dead.

But as much as time seems to be slipping away, it has also, in a bizarre sort of way, stood still. Like a child, I'm curled up on my bed on this lazy Friday morning on sleepy Cypress Lane, picturing things on the ceiling and the little rug on the floor. Above, I can see beasts, marvellous and strange, faces with mouths agape, electric guitars;

below, a story is taking place between rows of little men with pointed hats, fabulous winged creatures, and odd diamond shapes, in rows of red and white. Again, I can feel hot, heavy breaths condensing on my pillow in wet patches. Again, I find myself delighting in the numbness of my arms and the lightness that comes with it. Again, I can feel an oncoming of the shits, thinking about what has been and what will be. Again, I am hopelessly in love with a pretty girl with deep brown eyes who will never be mine, save in dreams and boyish meanderings of the mind. It is as if a page has been plucked from those days of unknowing and innocence; where was I then, and where am I now? Ten-year-old Asha lives yet; and, if I brush away the long black locks from my face, I can see him staring back at me in wonderment. I am happy those days now lie buried beneath dust and the shards of broken hearts and dreams; but shall I ever emerge? Whither, from here? How strange, to feel at once so old, and yet so young.

23

As a soft ray from the afternoon sun poured onto an old, faded *gelim,* washing it in a glowing, ephemeral light, Grandpa emerged from behind the cracked kitchen wall. It was precisely a quarter to three, the time when young love buds, only to wither and fade away. Outside, in the primary school on the opposite end of the narrow alley, little boys in hushed hues of ochre and olive filled the stifling air with shrill shouts of elation, as they tried their utmost to scurry about in the drabness of the concrete playground enclosed by walls in lifeless green. Save their juvenile clamour, Yazdani Street was relatively quiet. The faint sounds of honks and whizzing tyres from the main street a block away occasionally seeped through the clefts in the windowsill, and through the blinds, one could make out the swarthy, spectral shapes of bent old ladies gnawing at the corners of their black *chadors.*

It had been a while since I'd last paid Grandpa a visit, or even called him, so engrossed had I been in this boredom of mine. I enjoy my visits to his little flat right beside the old Italian restaurant on Yazdani Street, where he's been living for as long as I can remember, and from where he won't ever budge. I always feel like I'm in that diner scene in *Pulp Fiction* where the pretty blonde cokehead talks about that special someone with whom she can just be quiet without having to say anything. Grandpa is sort of like that. With Grandpa, I don't have to put on airs or appearances, or make small talk to break any awkward silences; it's all tea, biscuits, and old records, interrupted only by flashes of poetic inspiration here and there, and the odd harangue against the bearded ones. What do I have to say, anyway? Even *I* can't bear my own thoughts anymore, these words and images buffeting my brains in flurries. No, I'd rather not talk, and instead save my boozy breaths for those songs I sing softly for myself and the girl on the fifth floor, to the twang and rattle of my guitar and the rhythms driving in my brambly head, sitting by my window. Maybe it *is* nice, sometimes, to just shut the fuck up, like brother Tarantino said.

The crackly lament of Shajarian warbled forth from the squeaky old cassette player, while Grandpa tossed his head about in subdued fits of passion. 'Bah bah', he exclaimed under his yellowed whiskers from time to time. I don't get it. I could never dig these damned oldies and classical songs; I mourn enough as it is, for a wasted life and dreams dead before they ever bloomed, and the sound of these old farts weeping and wailing is the last thing I need. There's something so funereal about them, so harrowing and unsettling, just like the murals everywhere in the city. And, like those pallid pictures and ashen faces wasting away in the sky and those amorphous shapes of black, they're everywhere I go. We've been damned, from the very start, from those hallowed days when Rostam was still Rostam, to mourn, forever and always. Enough doom and gloom, enough despair; give the kids some rock and roll, I say. *Let the children lose it, let the children use it, and let all the children boogie.* Let's turn the amps up to eleven and paint the town red … Ah, that'll be the day.

Grandpa doesn't like rock and roll, and neither do Mum and Dad. It's just me and Auntie, and even she's become soft with age. I played Grandpa a Stones record once, and he wasn't pleased, to say the least; he deems it the work of Ahriman himself. That afternoon, Grandpa asked me if I was still playing 'those songs' on my guitar and listening to 'that music'. He, too, like Mum and Dad, is worried about me. The guitar, he thinks, can only lead to no good. First, it's the music and the hair; next will come shady friends and pockets full of pills, and ultimately, I'll end up at best a tawdry minstrel strung out on smack, the bane of the family and the boon of cheap wedding dos. He always looks at the old picture of Zoroaster beside that of the Shah and Farah, in its gilded frame on an embroidered spread resting atop the television, and throws up an old hand in despair, saying, 'God, grant all the young ones health and success!' What Grandpa doesn't know is that I've already developed quite the penchant for booze, as well as the occasional toke here and there, whenever the opportunity arises. They're not essential to rock and roll, though; I'm just attracted to the sweet numbness they bring. Come to think of it, I could go for a drink right about now; but no – it's only ten in the morning. Even a hound has his scruples.

Dad, on the other hand, sees things somewhat differently. The music he loved died along with the Revolution; I just listen to screams, shouts, and other sundry 'noises', as he likes to call them. For Baba, it's all about the greats: Googoosh, Hayedeh, Ebi, Farhad ... stuff you don't hear in the clubs, theatres, or streets anymore. He never cared for the Beatles or the Stones, and wouldn't exchange the sweet sound of his Persian tongue for anything. Even the old-timers still working in Tehrangeles or whatever other godforsaken city have lost it; gone are those flowery words, those sublime strings, the alchemy of an age hurtling headlong towards the abyss of the 80s. Ebi and Googoosh are all right, I guess; but I've always needed something ... *heavier* ... something with grinding guitars and a beat to get me up in my torn black kicks, strutting my stuff. Dad never cared for my rock stars with their long hair, bad teeth, and low-slung electric guitars; he lives yet with weary birds, lonely hearts, and flowers wrought of stone – and quite likes it, I think.

* * *

I was watching the little boys run hither and thither in their gummy white shoes, soaked in sweat yet still sipping on a glass of tea that scalded my fingers (as if obliged to), when Agha-ye Ghorbani, the little old humpbacked man next door, sounded the three damning tones of the intercom in which he appeared daubed in blurred blues. Mr. Ghorbani often visits Grandpa unexpectedly in his noisy plastic slippers and sweatpants pulled up to his chest to chew the fat and make small talk in his quaint Azeri accent. Not ever having the patience to speak with him (or having anything to say to him, for that matter), he likewise ignores me, aside from tossing a curt *salam* and downward glance. Without answering the intercom,

I opened the squeaky metal door outside in the *hayat* and told Grandpa I'd go for a nap in his bedroom. 'Basheh', he said, shaking his head with a sigh, knowing he'd lost his tea boy for the afternoon.

My white linen shirt, which I'd undone down to the third button (in the spirit of Keith) behind closed doors, had become so soiled with cool sweat that I had to keep my arms away from my sides. I remembered how, as a boy, I used to cherish that sour smell lingering on the shirts and jackets of the mustachioed ones at our *mehmoonis*; for it was, I thought, the smell of *men* – and a man is what I'd always wanted to be. I envied the older kids who reeked of fake cologne and who'd scrape their faces smooth with the razor blades they sell at the corner stores and street stalls I'd always look at with longing, as I paid for my soda pop and *Adams Khersi*. I wanted the pretty girls on Vali-ye Asr to take me seriously, and give me the same looks they gave the other boys. I never wanted to be a kid, and don't miss a single one of those days the old geezers keep telling me to cherish; I wanted to grow up as soon as possible and be a man, just like Mr. Keith Richards and my celluloid heroes. Imagine my joy, then, when I came home from school one day to find little dark patches underneath my t-shirt. *At last!* I thought. I pulled off my tee with excitement and smelled my underarms, relishing the scent of adulthood. *Just like ghormeh sabzi! Mmm …*

But sweating my arse off has long lost the tinge of romanticism it once held. In Grandpa's room, I threw my soaked shirt over an armchair covered in cracked leather, and myself on the bed. On his dresser lay a little picture of me as a toothy two-year-old, beside Grandma's old lipstick cartridges and pocket mirrors, which he'd arranged in exactly the same way, as if she could still see them. Again came those hot, slushy waves, those chills down low; I felt as if I were back in the old bookstore at the hotel. Like it, Grandpa's bedroom is a museum, a time machine, a washed-out snapshot of the seventies browning around the edges and reeking of mothballs. But then again, the past is all Grandpa has, all he can lean on. Everyone's either gone or moved away to some faraway land, while the Iran he knew and loved, like Dad's music, died in '79. Yet, Grandpa would never leave Iran for the world; he would be lost without his memories, without these sleepy back alleys and the shouts of the swarthy boys in the schoolyard. He calls those in Tehrangeles 'a bunch of traitors' and the ones in England spies who think they've fallen off an elephant's arse. I haven't told him about my rock and roll dreams yet, for I don't know what old Grandpa will make of them. Plastic and spy games aren't my scene; give me my battered cherry-red guitar and a seedy bar in Soho, and even Grandpa will be glad I left. 'That's my boy', he'll say, when he and all the neighbours see me on the television; and Mr. Ghorbani will sip on hot tea between abyssal sighs, cursing himself for not having gotten my autograph when he had the chance.

I busied myself with the pages of a comic book called *Regained Glory,* in which the Shah looked like some sort of superhero. I wasn't really reading it though, half-distracted as I was by the insufferable heat of the stuffy bedroom and Mr. Ghorbani's broken Persian that had me biting my cheeks to stifle a giggle here and there. He was, I reckon, telling Grandpa about his son in Germany who not only has two PhDs and an MBA, but a BMW, too, and specialises in piecing back together people who've fallen from dizzying heights and helicopters. And what did Grandpa have to say about his *agha pesar*? 'He's busy with school and all … he'll find his way sooner or later.' The only way I can see is *out*. I sometimes wonder what would have happened had the Shah – 'a most evil man', as our boyhood schoolbooks covered in flowers used to call him – not been driven out of Iran. I don't think he would have minded me and my guitar as much as this bearded bunch. Maybe I could have stayed here and seen a future for myself, maybe I … ah, but what's the use of all these 'maybes' and 'what ifs'? What's been done has been done. The question is, where do I go now? The voice of Mr. Ghorbani, who had almost given up on Persian altogether, cut through the bedroom door: 'May God keep the young ones!'

* * *

But the bastard wouldn't leave, so enthralled was he by the sound of his own voice and the fibs he was weaving with his sausage-like fingers into a tawdry *gelim* I imagined to be lined with little helicopters and BMWs. My blue jeans had become one with my sticky legs, but I didn't feel like taking them off, preferring instead to writhe about on Grandpa's thick, furry blanket and not think about how badly I had to pee. *Damn this place, and damn that tea,* I thought, wondering when Mr. Ghorbani would get his fat arse off the sofa and call it a day. Resigning myself to the fate of yet another cruel summer afternoon, I curled up into a ball of sweat and bones, and looked with lost eyes at the neatly arranged artefacts in Grandpa's little museum from 'those days'. I had become accustomed to Mr. Ghorbani's forked tongue, and could no longer sense the smell of mothballs. For a moment, I imagined myself as only a manifestation of being, feeling suspended in time and space and finding even the sound of my own name strange. But I soon resurfaced, although someplace else.

Ramesh was singing a song of temptation on the *Rangarang* show on a hazy Thursday night with the sun in its last throes, while Mum scurried about in noisy heels in a kitchen full of steam, trying to upturn a pot of *tahchin* into a consummately moulded cake, lest her trials amount to naught. Dad, in his bedroom, was cursing beneath his beery breath the red satin tie he always had difficulty tying into a knot, as well as the guests we were expecting and the 'whole damned *mehmooni* business'. I had just come home from the Niagara cinema, where, nervously washing down sunflower seeds with Coca Cola and occasionally glancing at the pretty girl two seats to my right, I watched Behrouz Vossoughi get beaten to a pulp like a right badass while an unknowing mariachi band played on throughout the night. I hadn't had my first kiss yet, but that afternoon, had tasted my first cigarette outside the schoolyard. I was trembling in my deep blue bellbottoms, for if Dad were to find out, I knew he'd have me hung and quartered. I didn't know whom I loved more: Behrouz, or Naser Malekmotiee. It didn't matter, though; Behrouz had Googoosh, and Naser always got Forouzan, so you'd win both ways. Although I cherished the long black hair that fell onto my shoulders, I played with the thought of getting it cropped, just like

Behrouz's. In the taxi on the way home, I decided I would put together just enough pocket money to be able to buy a sheepskin-lined denim jacket and some new black leather shoes. I might, I thought, even take up wrestling one day. You needed to be big and strong if you were going to get the dancing girl in the end.

Though she always complained that she could no longer smell it on herself, Mum had again put on her rosewater-scented perfume, and Dad, his Eau Sauvage, some of which I'd spray all over myself when he wasn't around, for the times I'd get together with the boys for a night on the town. Having put on a single I'd recently bought from Lame Ahmad's shop near Vanak Square, I jumped into a pair of chequered trousers and tried to get my hair to fall on my brow in just the right way, tossing it to and fro, while Kambiz sang of the ways of love to the quavering inflections of heaven. Even before I slipped into my new white button-down shirt, I broke out in a cool, mild sweat, thinking about the girls who might come to the gathering. I never knew who'd show up – a distant cousin, a relative's friend, someone wholly unknown altogether – and so I was always on my toes. Perhaps the girl from the cinema would be there in her red leather shoes and short black skirt, I thought, or someone even prettier; whatever happened would probably be for the best. I hadn't yet had my fill of beer, of which Mum and Dad would let me have a little on Thursday nights (they didn't know I had it all the time), yet already felt heady just thinking about the hours ahead. I knew that anything could happen, that I might fall in love, or, even more exciting, that someone might fall in love with *me*. I imagined how we might slip, amidst the banter and confusion, back into my bedroom and lose ourselves in each other's embrace, smothering one another with kisses while I'd try to fight an oncoming hard-on born not of lust, but the thrill of love and feeling so *alive*. Though we'd prick up our ears lest we be rudely interrupted, if anyone happened to chance upon us, I'd tell them I only wanted to show her my record collection and the pictures on my wall. We would think ourselves lucky to be in Tehran, the most happening place we knew, fearing nothing but the dwindling hours of the night and the hand of dawn, which might part us forevermore.

Yet, even as I stood there, half-dressed before my bedroom mirror, as the notes warbled on and the poet pondered the passing of time, all those languid gazes seemed but reflections of a dream, of Arezu's deep brown eyes.

24

The orange orb overhead, swirling suspended atop heads of white, burns still with all of August's vehemence, though in the descendent and heedless of the lion's beck from afar. It will sink, slowly, into the shadows, into the splinters of the night, into the black abyss of Ahriman, surfacing only in the meagre hours of dying days and the hearts of those who hold it dear, as they await with heavy eyes a dark December's eve. Summer, it once seemed, would never end, like Jamshid's little book and the call to prayer on state television in flashes of green; but memories of July have all but slipped from my mind, and, sitting here on Mum's floral-patterned couch, downing tepid cups of instant coffee and waiting for the Stones to come on the television, I will soon bid August farewell. She will follow the immortal ones, those whose hearts were cleft in twain by the ravages of the earth, towards higher climes, leaving us all – me, the mountains obscured but undaunted by veils of smoke, the pin-ups on my bedroom wall. Is it strange that, somehow, I don't want these damning days to end? I never thought I'd find myself clutching at them with sweaty hands, as if to stop them from sliding beneath that silken sheet that shrouds everything in white, only leaving one with swirls and a canvas of a thousand fuzzy colours. August and its blues have come to an end; what will I make of September? And what will it make of me?

More semesters, more exams, more trials by fire. First, they asked me what I *wanted* to be. Then, they told me what I *had* to be. Now, they tell me I'll *never* be anyone or thing. There are tests to be failed, hearts to be broken, souls to be destroyed, and a few shining stars to be moulded of sweat, blood, and hysteria. On top of the usual, I'll have to see Babak every goddamn day and withstand the onslaught of a spate of daggers hurled at my breast, and of course, the shits. My teachers will question my upbringing and shake their balding heads in disapproval, and I'll while away those bitter mornings drawing little electric guitars of all shapes and sizes in the curled margins of my notebooks, with Friday (and booze) on my mind, and the cover of the next rock and roll record to smear with my inky fingers shining brightly before my eyes. On Thursday nights, the boys will go for liver sandwiches and cheap thrills, writing numbers on little scraps of paper and cruising around in heaving white cars. There will be drunken glances, sweet nothings, and the imprints of dripping red lips on teenage hearts. I will either be at home with my records, VH1, and my guitar, or at some *mehmooni* or other, where there will be no pretty girls to divert my thoughts, and people will ask me what I want to be in life. Knowing they'll laugh at me if I tell them the truth, or give a curt 'aha' at best, I won't tell them that I want to be a rock and roll star in London, but rather, spew out a textbook answer that will have them clinking their glasses against mine. 'You want to become an engineer? *Afarin bar to!*' I will loathe them all. I will feel weak in the knees, and wish for whatever rug I'm standing on to swallow me whole within its floral sprays and effulgent spheres. I will hate them, but deep down inside, admit that they're probably right to laugh. A rock star in London? *How?*

Scrambled flurries of black and white are all I can see. Snarling Mr. Richards and his butterscotch blonde are nowhere in sight, and the sweet nausea of *Avalon* seems further away than even Soho. It was only a matter of time before the men in green would do the rounds again, gathering up the mirrors of Paradise baking patiently above our roofs, pulling the cord on the hopes and dreams of boys whose only solace is the image of a scruffy man in skinny jeans throwing around an electric guitar with a cigarette burning between his blackened lips. I now only have state television, with its prick in the red hat to take me for a dimwit and stern warnings of hellfire and laments for all the young dudes. Bolan tells us to have hope; he says they won't fool us, *no no.* But they did fool us, and now they've fucked us. After high school has chewed and spat me out, they'll come for my beloved *kakol,* just like they did my heroes. But they'll have to run after me with all their might; this little hound can bark and bite. No, it can't end that way; T. Rex speaks the truth. They won't fool me into thinking there isn't anything beyond all of this, that there isn't a way out. There is … there *has* to be. I have more faith than I give myself credit for.

I'm not having any of it. I've made up my mind: I will go and see Big Behnam, after Mad Manuch gets me *Diamond Dogs.* They'll smuggle me out of here, *kakol* and all, to Turkey. I've heard Istanbul is nice. I'll do some odd jobs here and there and scrape together enough dough to get my skinny arse to London Town. I'm not bad at washing dishes, and think I could pull off some office work as well. There, I'll get a place of my own in Soho, where I can play my records and my guitars as loud as I want. I'll find myself a drummer and a bassist, and will form the Afghan Hounds, the greatest rock and roll band England will have seen since the Stones. Keith Richards will read about me in the papers, and will want to meet the Persian cat who can make his electric guitar howl like no one else. I will see Keef there, as I will Mick and Ziggy. I will ask Bryan Ferry whether *Avalon* gives him the shits as well, or if it's just me. I will make it there, and laugh at the thought of all my teachers rotting away in the same crumbling high school building and watching me on satellite television at night, cursing me and wishing they were me at once. I'll show them what this raven-haired hound in his blue jeans and torn little kicks can do. The whole lot of them.

* * *

Sounds beckon from beyond the jagged threshold of the Alborz Mountains, sounds strange and sublime, whispering through the stringy locks blanketing my ears. The workers with the piercing eyes are gone, along with their rusty blue pickup truck. Mum and Dad have yet to come home, and sleepy Cypress Lane lies demure, awash in splashes of pink, which taste, I imagine, as the pretty girl on the fifth floor smells. She will never be mine, not now, not ever. There are songs unsung, words unread, and rattling riffs that have drowned in folds of silence. The coffee is cold, and not a drop of the good stuff is to be found beneath the kitchen sink. I've got the shits again, brought on this time not by the man in white, but the thought of August's end and the coming of the new school term. The starman has flown back, behind this ruddy haze of soot and exhaust, into the sky; look hard enough, and you will see his face not in the pastel moon, but in a trembling white spark of light. He knows, like me, that this is no place for longhaired rock and rollers and their electric dreams, which only fizzle out into nothingness.

But as much as the world weighs down on my little soul here, as much as I loathe it all and know I must leave, something tells me I'm going to miss Tehran, these boring, burning afternoons, these slow rushes, and those faraway eyes, with all my heart.

GLOSSARY OF NAMES, EXPRESSIONS, AND TERMS

Afarin	Bravo. Afarin bar to = 'good on you'
Ahsant	Bravo
Agha	A male honorific of Turkic origin; the Persian equivalent of 'sir'
Ahriman	The Iranian/Zoroastrian equivalent of Satan
Akh	A sound used to imply a sigh
Azizam	Lit. 'my dear'
Baba	An informal word for 'father'
Bah bah	My my
Basheh	OK
Chador	A body-length cloth covering worn by religious Iranian women. The word also means 'tent' in Persian
Chai	Tea
Degh kard	He/she died of depression/heartache. It is also casually used to imply a mild form of misery (e.g. degh kardam = 'I'm so down')
Ey vay	An expression of astonishment or dismay that roughly translates to 'oh no'
Fatwa	A religious edict in Islam issued by an Ayatollah
Gelim	A tribal Iranian carpet

Ghermezi	'Reddy' (from the Persian ghermez, meaning 'red')
Giveh	A traditional Iranian slipper
Hayat	A courtyard in a traditional Iranian house
Heyvan	Animal
Hejab	Headscarf
Ist	Lit. 'stop'
Jadeh Ghadim	Lit. 'The Old Road'
Kachal	Bald
Kakol	Forelock
Kaleh Pacheh	Sheep's head and trotters, a popular Iranian dish usually eaten for breakfast
Khanum	A female honorific of Turkic origin; the Persian equivalent of 'Miss'
Khoda	God. Khodaya / Ey Khoda = 'Oh God'
Mehmooni	An informal group gathering, usually held for leisure at one's house
Mohandes	Engineer
Ney	An Iranian reed flute
Norooz	The Iranian New Year, celebrated at the time of the vernal equinox. Norooz literally means 'New Day', and is celebrated not only in Iran, but also by Iranian peoples (e.g. Afghans, Kurds, Tajiks, etc.) around the world
Pasdar	Lit. 'preserver'. Pasdars are the Revolutionary Guards of the Islamic Republic of Iran
Pesar	Boy
Salam	Hello
Setar	A long-necked Iranian lute commonly

	used in classical music. Setar, literally, means 'three strings'
Tahchin	A traditional Iranian dish known for its distinctive cake-like shape and yellow colour
Toman	A unit of Iranian currency. 10 rials (the rial being the lowest denomination of currency in Iran) are equivalent to one toman
Zan Daei	The wife of one's maternal uncle
Zan-Zalil	A term used to describe a helpless man who gives in to his wife (or girlfriend's) every whim
Zoghali Burger	A popular fast-food chain in Iran. Zoghal in Persian means 'charcoal'